Murder With a Hint of Cinnamon

Kristy T Dixon

For Michelle Clark and Katie Thompson

Chapter 1

The new sign above the diner looked incredible. I shaded my eyes with one hand and smiled. The sign now read Sue's Diner. Gramma Sue's diner was now restored to its former glory, and the Linda's Diner sign was in the big dumpster behind the building. It looked nice above the red-and-white awning.

"Ivy! That looks amazing!" Boyd Webster said, crossing the street toward me. He patted me on the shoulder, and we stood looking at the sign. Boyd had been one of my strongest supporters since I moved to Muddy Creek three months ago. He was like the grandpa I never knew I needed.

"It does look good, doesn't it?"

"Sure does. Your Gramma Sue would be proud. When is the grand reopening?"

"Saturday. I'm a little nervous, but I'm not sure why."

He rubbed a hand over his mostly bald head. "No need to be nervous. I think everyone's looking forward to it. I know I've missed your cookies."

"I should make you some. I have time today."

"Don't feel like you have to go out of your way for me."

I pulled him into a side hug. "I love making things for people who appreciate them."

He chuckled. "That's me for sure, and I bet the sheriff might come around for a chance at a cookie."

Creepers rubbed around my ankles, and I picked him up. He purred when I began rubbing his soft gray fur. "The sheriff has been pretty busy wrapping everything up with Uncle Rob's murder. I'm not sure a cookie will get him over here."

"Things will calm down, and he'll be back."

It sounded like Boyd was trying to reassure me. I wasn't sure why. The sheriff and I were only friends, after all. Sheriff Jett Malone was the best-looking man in Muddy Creek and one of the nicest, but I knew better than to set my sights on him.

"Have you seen José?" I asked. "I know he's supposed to be back in town before the opening, but he hasn't texted me in a couple of days."

Boyd nodded. "He got back to town late last night."

"Oh good. We can't have a grand opening without him." José was the head cook. I knew he was looking forward to the opening. When he worked for my aunt Linda, he was limited in what he could cook. There had been a set thing for each meal with no menu choices. Now that I owned the diner, José and I had come up with a real menu, and I couldn't wait to see how the town reacted to it. It wasn't as big as a menu in a big city, but anything would be an improvement.

Creepers wiggled in my arms, so I placed him on the ground. He went up to the door and meowed. Creepers likes his bed on the windowsill, and he only tolerates being outside for a short time.

"Did you hire more people?" Boyd asked.

"A few."

"I bet you need more than a few."

Boyd was probably right. Linda's Diner only had two cooks and three servers because that was all they needed. Now that the menu was expanded, we would need more employees. It was my hope anyway. As the only place in town that served food, even Linda's limited menu brought people in. In my fantasies, people flocked here to see the changes.

"I hired Darcy Peterson to cook. That still only gives us two cooks since Larry is gone. I also hired a couple of teenagers to wait tables. If it looks like we need more, I can scale up. I don't want to hire too many and have to let anyone go."

"That's smart."

Creepers was scratching on the wooden doorframe, so I said goodbye to Boyd and let the tired cat inside. As soon as the door opened, he shot through the diner and up the steps to our room. I followed him to open the door. He scurried across the floor and jumped onto the windowsill.

I looked around my room and smiled. The room wasn't huge, but it looked a lot nicer than it had when I first got here. I had been sleeping on the floor and then on a mattress on the floor. Now I had a decent bed and dresser, and I'd decorated the walls with framed pictures of Agatha Christie book covers. I sat on the window seat and rubbed Creepers's back.

"It looks so much better in here. Don't you think so?"

Creepers batted at me with his paw. He wanted me to leave him to his nap.

"Fine," I said. "If you don't want my company, I'll go down and make Boyd his cookies." I gave him a final pat and went to the kitchen. The kitchen was off the dining area, and a wall separated the two rooms. The large rectangular window had a wide ledge on which to place the food. It was the best way to watch what was going on from the kitchen and pass food through. I glanced at the broken jukebox in the corner and wondered if it was fixable. Even when Gramma Sue ran the diner, it hadn't worked.

I flipped on the kitchen light and got the mixer ready. It was hard to believe how much my life had changed in the past few months. I'd only come to Muddy Creek as a favor to my aunt, and I hadn't planned on staying. Now, the diner was mine, and I'd made a few friends along the way.

I pulled my long blond hair into a ponytail and stuffed it into a hairnet. The last thing I needed was to have strands of hair in my cookies. That would be a terrible way to advertise my baking. I pulled on an ugly white apron and cringed. That was something I should replace. The servers all had pretty purple aprons, but the cooks had faded, ugly white ones.

Baking is a passion of mine. I rarely cook meals, but I love to make desserts. My mom and I started baking together when I was too young to remember. It kept us close throughout my high school and college years.

I hummed while I mixed the dough. I only do that when no one is in the diner. I can't sing or hum in tune. Heck, I can't even whistle in tune. Creepers puts up with it, so it's our little secret. It wasn't long before I had the first two batches in the oven. While I was cleaning, I heard the doorbell. I had one installed now that I'm living here.

I rushed to open the door and smiled when I saw the sheriff through the glass. His brown hair was messy, and he was yawning. I pulled open the door and grinned. "Hi, Jett. It's been a while."

He scratched at the stubble on his chin. "Yeah, I've been catching up on paperwork and had to go to court a few times."

He didn't tell me any details from the trial. I'd told him I didn't want to know. I'd helped solve my uncle's murder, and I was ready to move on. Testifying wasn't something I would be able to get out of, but I hoped it was a quick thing.

"I'll have some cookies out of the oven in a few minutes. Do you want to come in?"

He grinned. "I was hoping you would say something like that. My mom occasionally makes cookies, but they don't compare to yours."

I let him in and led him to the kitchen. It only just struck me that the sheriff had a family. As far as I know, I'd never met them. In fact, I knew very little about Jett's personal life. "Do you live with your parents?"

He chuckled. "No. When I got this job, my mom offered to let me stay with them, but I need my own space. The sheriff shouldn't have his mom telling him to make his bed."

I pushed the oven light and glanced in at the cookies. "You don't make your bed?"

He sat on a stool, and his eyes sparkled. "Not as a rule. I'm just going to mess it up later. Hey, I heard you got Darcy to work for you. Can she cook?"

"I hope so," I said, turning off the beeping timer and pulling out a tray of cookies. "She says she can. She was going to move to Topeka for a job, but when I told her I was hiring, she decided to stay. If she moved, she wouldn't have anyone to watch Netty."

Jett frowned. "I wish she didn't have to leave Netty with her mom. Sally isn't the best influence."

"She's not going to work the dinner shift unless necessary. She'll be here when Netty is at school. I told her she can bring her in if she has to work late."

Jett's frown turned to a smile. "You look thrilled about that."

I laughed. "I can only imagine Netty sitting at the bar judging me with her cute little eyes. I still can't believe she wanted you to arrest me for sneezing."

"Don't take it personally. She's probably tried to get me to arrest everyone in town at least once."

I grabbed the spatula and placed the cookies onto the cooling rack. "I believe it."

Jett grabbed a cookie, and I watched it bend and fall apart all over his hands. I'd scolded him more than once about eating piping-hot cookies, so now it was on him. If he wanted burned fingers, it was his choice. I went to the fridge and pulled out a gallon of milk. I poured two glasses and handed one to him.

"Thanks," he said, washing his cookie down with a big gulp of milk. "I heard you donated a ton of books to the library."

I shrugged. "I'm glad they can go to a good cause. I never get rid of books, so I have a lifetime's worth at my mom's place. She was only too happy to ship a bunch of them over here. Most of them are from my younger days."

"*Nancy Drew*?"

I gasped dramatically. "Why don't you make me get rid of Agatha Christie while you're at it? *Nancy Drew* is not something I'm parting with. I'm thinking of rereading them. I don't have space to put books while I'm here, or I would have them all."

"Whoa, whoa, whoa," Jett said, standing. "What do you mean while you're here? I thought you were staying."

"Oh, I am. I don't know if I'll live above the diner forever, though. Maybe for a year or two."

"Good. You scared me for a minute."

My mouth turned up. "Yeah, your life would go back to being boring if I left."

He laughed. "You haven't gotten into trouble in a while. At least, not that I'm aware of."

"I figure you needed a break."

"When you asked me about Darcy's husband a while back, I worried you were going to run around town trying to find out what happened to him."

I grabbed a cookie and took a bite. It was too hot, but I forced myself not to react. I was going to try to figure out what happened to him. Darcy had asked me to. I was no detective, but I was determined and not too bad at solving a mystery here and there.

"Oh no," he groaned. "You're going to, aren't you? I can see it in your eyes."

I leaned against the counter and smiled. "Don't worry about it. It's not your case, so I won't get in your way."

"You shouldn't put yourself in danger."

"What makes you think it will be dangerous? Everyone around here seems to think he ran away. If that's what happened, it shouldn't be a problem."

He sighed and took another cookie. "I wasn't around when he disappeared. I find it all hard to believe, though."

"Why?"

"He had a wife and a kid. His job was decent, and people said he seemed happy. Why would a guy like that disappear? If it was just an awful marriage, wouldn't his parents know where he was? Darcy said he hadn't been in contact with them."

"Has Darcy ever asked you to look into it?" I asked.

"Nope."

"Hmm." As soon as the diner reopened, I was going to dive into this.

Jett shook his head. "You have that look again. Whatever you do, be careful. And take José. And possibly Boyd. I can't believe I'm saying that."

"Of course, I'll take them." José and Boyd had helped me solve my uncle's murder. José was fifty and in fairly good shape. Boyd was closer to seventy and served as a lookout. We might not be the obvious choice for solving mysteries, but we had succeeded. I laughed to myself. I was thinking we were some official detectives and not a few random people who had solved one crime.

"Don't do anything you shouldn't."

I smirked. "Like what?"

"No sneaking into places or talking to shady characters. Nothing dangerous." He grinned. "Then call me when you break the rules, and I'll come save you."

"Ha ha. If I remember correctly, you were the one who got punched in the face and tackled."

He took a gulp of milk. "You got me there. You got that scar, though."

I touched the spot on my cheek that now had a thin white line going across it. It was fading nicely, and I hoped it wouldn't be noticeable in a few months. "That was from my clumsiness, so it doesn't count."

He shook his head. "Just be careful. Alright?"

"Sure."

Chapter 2

"If I grow a goatee, do I have to wear a hairnet on my face?" José asked as he mixed some batter. It was Saturday morning, and the diner was opening in ten minutes.

I tilted my head and grinned at him. "I'm not sure. I'd have to google it. Isn't there something about it when you apply for a food handler's permit?"

"I don't remember."

"I think they call them beard covers," Darcy said. "When I took the test, there was something about it."

José sighed. "Then I guess I'll keep shaving. I don't think that would be very comfortable. It's bad enough I have to cover my fabulous hair." I grinned. José's black hair was always slicked back and neatly combed.

My stomach was in knots. "Are you two ready for this?" I asked. "People are already lined up outside. It's going to be crazy."

"I've been waiting for this since I started here," José said. "I'm glad I can finally make things people want to eat."

"Your food was good before," Darcy said, turning on the skillet.

"Yes, but now people can choose what they want. It's more of a challenge."

"Are you all ready out there?" I asked, poking my head through the window that went into the seating area.

The five servers all turned to look at me. They were doing one last check to make sure things were tidy.

"We're ready," Livy said, straightening her purple apron. Elle and Trina looked a little uncertain, but they were new.

"You'll all be great!" I said, pulling my head back into the kitchen.

"Do you think we have enough servers?" José asked.

"I hope so. I hired everyone who applied, so if we need more, it might be hard."

"I bet we need another cook, too."

"We probably won't know until the novelty wears off. I bet today is crazy. I hope I made enough dessert."

José chuckled. "I think you made enough to feed three towns. I'm not worried about running out."

"I hope Netty behaves while I'm gone," Darcy muttered. "She drives my mom crazy."

"You could have brought her."

"No, it's too long of a day for her."

I was pretty sure I would become quick friends with Darcy. She was around thirty-five, so she was about five years older than me, but not enough to matter. I laughed to myself. If she became my friend, she would be the youngest one I'd made in Muddy Creek.

"I'm going to open the door," I said, taking a deep breath. I had no reason to be nervous. Most of the people I'd met here had been nice enough. Even if they hated it, they would probably still be polite.

I walked to the front door and turned the lock. I hoped they didn't all come rushing in and squish me. Sheriff Malone was in the front, and next to him was Barbra. Everyone was excited. Not a lot happened around here.

"Welcome, everyone!" I called. "Thank you for being here! Come on in."

I stepped back and let them enter. Barbra squeezed my arm. "It looks great, kiddo."

I smiled and let Livy lead her to a table. Her hair was light purple this week. She had told me that colorful hair made her feel fifty instead of seventy-five.

A lot of people poured into the diner. Way more than we had space for.

"Hi, neighbors," I said above the noise. "We have some tables set up out back if any of you are willing to sit outside. If you are, let us know." I went into the kitchen and tried not to panic. "There are a ton of people out there."

Darcy nodded. "It's a good thing José suggested the outside tables."

"Yes, it is." I never would have thought of it, and I hadn't been super excited about the idea at first. The diner didn't have any buildings behind it, just the flat Kansas prairie. The view wasn't ideal, but José argued that everyone here was used to it. It would be beautiful for the people who came at sunset. Kansas had the prettiest sunsets I'd ever seen. For the rest of the day, the view would be of tall, dying grass.

"What if it stays like this all day? I thought breakfast would be slower, and lunch and dinner would have enormous crowds."

José glanced out of the kitchen. "Everyone's just excited. I'm sure it will die down in a few days."

"I hope so. We want to have a lot of customers, but not more than we can handle." I heard a meow and looked down to see Creepers. "You can't be in the kitchen, buddy." I scooped him up and took him upstairs. I would let him run around the diner, but I worried about how customers would feel about that.

I put him in my room and gave him a quick cuddle. "You never want to come downstairs. Do you feel like you're missing out today?" If he was going to start getting out, I would need a bigger space. Maybe staying at the diner hadn't been my best idea.

The day went by better than I could have hoped. We had a steady stream of people all day and only a few mishaps. By the time we closed the doors, I was exhausted. It took over an hour to clean up even though we had tried to clean as we went throughout the day.

"You were all awesome," I told my employees. "I think I'm going to hire a couple of teenagers to come in to clean. It would save us all a lot of time. Can you all spread that around?"

"I know a few people who might be interested," Livy said.

"Have them come talk to me. We should probably find someone who can also be here during the day to keep up with the dishes. And don't worry. Today was crazy, but I won't be expecting you all to work all day, every day."

"What will our hours be on school days?" Elle asked, pulling a hairband from her black braids. "My mom will only let me work a few hours a day during school."

"Of course," I said, wondering why I hadn't thought of school. That would only leave Livy and Sarah who could work during the day. The others were still in high school and could only work a few hours a day. I probably needed at least two shifts since we were open for twelve hours. That was too long for anyone. José had been working terrible hours the entire time he worked for my aunt. I needed to fix this.

"I bet the crowds will drop off in a few days," José said, running water over a pan. "I think we'll stay busier than when it was Linda's, but it will still be manageable when people are at work and school."

I sighed. It wouldn't be easy to find people to work here. The town was so small. "Why don't you all leave? I can finish this." I didn't want everyone quitting because of the long day.

Everyone left except José and Darcy. By the time we finished, I was ready to drop. I'd only been able to escape a few times to check on Creepers, and he probably missed me.

"Have you decided whether you can try to help me find Patrick?" Darcy asked as she put away the last pan. "I know you're busy."

I stifled a yawn. "I'll try. Sorry I haven't gotten back to you. Things have been crazy."

"That's alright. And I can pay you."

I knew she was being polite. I'd heard about her mother's money problems. "You don't have to pay me. I don't even know if I'll be any help."

José threw a rag into the laundry basket. "What's going on here?"

Darcy's eyes jumped to José. She must have forgotten he was there.

"Can José help me?" I asked. "He was useful when I was trying to find Rob's murderer."

Darcy nodded. "Yes, that's fine."

José tossed his apron. "What am I helping with?"

"Finding out what happened to my husband."

José's eyes widened. "Ohhh. I could help."

"What do I need to know?" I asked, grabbing a notepad and a pencil.

Darcy sank onto a stool. "His name was, I mean, is, Patrick Henderson. Here's a picture," she said, handing it to me. "You can keep it." I glanced at the picture. A man with red hair and green eyes stared up at me. He had freckles and a thin face.

"So he just disappeared one day?"

"Yes. People around here think he ran off, but I'll never believe it. I started going by Peterson again because everyone was so judgmental, and I'm weak. I wish I hadn't."

"Do you have any ideas about what happened?"

Darcy twisted her hairnet in her hands. "Not really. He went to work one day and never came home."

"Did he have any enemies?"

"No. He was a likable guy. He wasn't from Muddy Creek, and he only lived here for a short time. Most people around here didn't know him well."

"Where did he work?"

"Wichita. He commuted so I could live close to my mom. She needs a lot of help with her drinking and all. He worked for a communications company. I'm not exactly sure what he did, but it always sounded a little boring."

"So he just disappeared, and no one looked for him?"

"Basically. I got the police to check some things out, but I don't think they tried hard. They searched for his car, but nothing came of it."

"There were some rumors," José said softly.

She rolled her eyes. "Yes, from Matt Hooper. I think that's part of the reason no one took it seriously."

"Hooper? Is he related to Brian?" I asked. Brian was the town librarian and the person who gave me Creepers. He was one of the nicest guys I'd ever met.

"They're brothers," she said. "I dated Matt in high school. He didn't get over our break-up very well. Even though I didn't date Patrick until years after we broke up, he still spread rumors about him. He didn't even know him, but he told people that Patrick was no good and just using me. I think that's why the sheriff at the time figured he just ran off."

"Matt and Brian are as different as two brothers can be," José said.

Darcy nodded in agreement. "Matt is alright unless you make him mad. Then he never gets over it."

"I've never met him. Does he still live around here?"

"He has a house in Wichita," José said. "He keeps a house here and comes around occasionally, but I haven't seen him in a while.

"How long has it been since Patrick disappeared?" I asked.

"Five years."

"That's a long time."

Darcy pressed her lips together. "I know. I also know that makes everything harder. Deep down, I think he's probably dead, but I need to know. If he wasn't, he would have contacted his parents."

"Who was the last person to see him?"

"Me. He left for work and never came home. When I called his boss, he said he'd never come in that day. He usually carpooled, but the man he drove with was sick."

"Who was that?"

"Karl Lattmire. They didn't work at the same place, but it was on the same street."

José nodded. "I know Karl. He's a quiet guy. He doesn't live far from here."

"Did Patrick have any siblings?"

"One brother, but he's in jail. I've never even met him."

"Did they have a good relationship?"

"I don't know. Patrick didn't want to talk about him. His parents don't either. I don't even know his name."

"Is there anything else we should know?" I asked.

"Not that I can think of."

"It's not a lot to go on, but we'll try," I told Darcy.

"Thank you. Don't worry. I know it's a long shot. I won't blame you if nothing comes of it."

I nodded. That made me feel better. I was a little stressed about the whole thing. I didn't want Darcy to have bad feelings toward me if I couldn't figure it out.

Later that night, I lay in bed with Creepers curled up against my head. I wasn't sure where to begin. José and Boyd might be helpful. They had known Patrick. I was still getting a feel for the town, and even though it was small, there were still a lot of people I didn't know. Creepers stuck his paw over my face, and I eased to the side.

I would start with Brian Hooper at the library on Monday. With luck, he would be willing to talk about his brother, Matt, and I would go from there. I could go straight to Matt since he was the one who dated Darcy, but I'd never met him so that might be awkward. After I learned more about Matt, I would talk to the carpool buddy. I couldn't remember his name right now, and it was too dark to look at the notepad. It might be smart to speak with Sally Peterson as well. Darcy's mom wasn't the most pleasant person I'd ever met, but she wasn't scared to give her opinion.

I rolled over and tried to focus on sleep. I would be worthless tomorrow if I didn't get good sleep. Tomorrow was Sunday and the only day of the week the diner was closed, so I could sleep in if I wanted. I'm not usually the type of person to sleep in, though. I usually pop up at five thirty and can't go back to sleep.

Still, if I went to sleep now, I could catch up on some reading tomorrow. I was in the middle of a new book, and it was taking me longer than usual to read it because of everything that had been happening with the diner. If I could have a restful Sunday, my mind would be ready to go on Monday, and that was what Darcy needed from me.

Chapter 3

I love my window seat. I think I saw too many coffee commercials as a little girl, so now I sit by the window with my cat on my lap, a book in one hand, and hot chocolate in the other. It's really too warm for hot chocolate, but I drink it in the morning. With October just around the corner, I hope the mornings will start getting cooler.

Reading like this may look like a cozy commercial, but, in reality, it's hard to read while holding a cat, a mug of hot chocolate, and a book. I have a feeling I'm going to keep doing it, though. I might need to invest in a small table to set my drink on now that I have money.

Having money is strange. I'd never felt super poor, but when I came here, I had just lost my job and was living off my savings. Now, I had a monthly allowance that had belonged to my uncle, and even though I split it with my parents, it was still more money than I'd ever had. I also had money in the bank from selling my uncle's house. I felt a little guilty that I had come out so nicely.

The doorbell chimed, and I reluctantly put down my book and hot chocolate. I nudged Creepers, and he grudgingly climbed off my lap and onto the windowsill. A doorbell camera would be ideal. I hurried down the steps and across the diner and smiled when I saw Brian Hooper. He was saving me a trip tomorrow.

"Hey, Brian," I said, opening the door.

He pushed a hand over his curly black hair and grinned. "Hi. I was in the city yesterday, so I missed your grand opening." He held up a bag. "I got this for you."

I looked at it. "What is it?"

"Toys for Creepers."

I smiled and took the bag. "Thank you. You need to stop buying him things, though. You're going to spoil him rotten."

"I know, but it makes me happy."

I couldn't fault him for that. Brian's cat was Creepers's mom, and he loved cats more than anyone I'd ever known.

Creepers came lazily over to us. He had spent his first few months with Brian and always turned up when he heard his voice.

"Hey, buddy," Brian said, coming into the diner and scooping up my cat. Creepers purred and rested against him.

I closed the door and placed the bag on a table. "He still loves you."

"I'm glad you could take him so I can still see him."

"Me too. I wish I could get him interested in more things," I said, glancing into the bag. "I thought younger cats were a lot more hyper, but he seems happy to sit around most of the day."

"They all have their own personalities. You should be happy he isn't crawling up your furniture and breaking things."

"He scratched up the side of my dresser, but not too bad. I got him a cat tree, and he won't touch it."

"There's some catnip spray in the bag. Squirt it on the cat tree, and it might make him appreciate it more."

"I'll have to try that. I bought him a harness and leash, but he wants nothing to do with it. It would be fun to go on walks with him. I would try harder, but since he doesn't like to go out, it's probably a waste of time. It would be fun, though."

"I had a cat that would walk on a leash once. It takes patience for sure. It's best if you start when they are really little."

"Hey, someone was telling me you have a brother. I don't think I've ever met him." I'm not great at transitioning to new topics.

Some of the sparkle left Brian's eye, but then returned. "If you saw him, you would remember. He's taller than

I am, and the second-best-looking black man in Muddy Creek."

I laughed. "With you being the first."

He winked. "Of course. Matt likes to do his own thing. He doesn't really like Muddy Creek, so I'm not sure why he keeps a house here. He probably only stays in it three weeks a year. You know I told you about all the money I inherited? He inherited a lot as well, so I'm surprised he does nothing with his life. He just sits around and hopes Darcy Peterson will finally take him back."

"I'd heard they dated."

"Seventeen years ago. You would think he could move on after all this time. I'm not being completely fair. Matt is a lot better than he used to be. He's learned to control his anger and is thinking about returning to college. He used to say there was no point when he already had money. I think the boredom is finally getting to him."

"I hope he figures things out."

"Me too."

"Did you know Darcy's husband?"

"Yeah, Patrick was a good guy. I know people want to say otherwise, but I know people, and he was a good one. Matt hated him, of course, but he never gave him a chance."

I leaned against the table. "I wonder what happened to him."

"I don't know, but I can't imagine it was anything good. I feel bad for Darcy. She's pretty now, but you should have seen her before Patrick disappeared. She was enchanting, one of those people who draws people in with their cheerful personalities. Living with her mom has sucked the life from her. I heard you hired her. I hope that helps get some of her spark back."

"Me too. I really like her. Do you want a cookie? I have some leftovers from yesterday."

Brian flashed his perfect white teeth. "I've never said no to a cookie."

"Me neither," I said, leading him to the kitchen. I really should stop eating so many. Now that I stopped teaching my Zumba class, I wasn't getting the workout I should be. I opened up a large container full of cookies, and he put Creepers down and pulled out a few.

I grabbed a freezer bag. "I can give you a bag to take home if you want."

He bit his cookie. "That would be great, thanks. Hey, I have a question for you. You told me you'd always wanted a cat, and you'd already picked out a name when you were young. Why Creepers? I'm not bashing it. I'm just curious."

I looked at Creepers and shrugged. "It's short for Cosmic Creepers."

He stared blankly at me.

"You know, from *Bedknobs and Broomsticks*?" I put some cookies in the bag and handed it to him.

"Ohhh. I haven't seen that movie in years. I don't even remember the cat having a name."

The doorbell chimed again. "I'm popular today," I said. "I'll be right back."

"I should be going." Brian followed me to the front door. "Looks like the sheriff."

I opened the door. "Hey, Jett."

"Hi," he said. He was holding a bag in one hand. "How's it going, Brian?"

"Good. How about you?"

"Fine." Jett stared at Brian and didn't say anything else.

There was an uncomfortable silence, then Brian squeezed past him. "I'll see you both later."

I waved. "Bye, Brian!"

"See you."

Jett closed the door. Everything felt awkward, but I wasn't sure why.

"Does Brian come over often when the diner is closed?"

"No," I said, "This was the only time. He brought some toys for Creepers." Creepers meowed and rubbed around Jett's ankles. Jett leaned down and ran his hand over the cat's back, and Creepers closed his eyes.

"Why?"

"I got Creepers from Brian. He's still attached to him and likes to see him. It's really sweet."

"Brian loves his cats. He would probably have a hundred if it were allowed."

"What's in the bag?" I asked, pointing.

He smiled. "I wanted to give you this yesterday, but I forgot to bring it to the opening." He pulled out some material and handed it to me. I took it and unfolded it. It was an apron. An apron covered in cats. "I know you hate those white aprons, so I thought I should get you one that fits your personality better."

A laugh wanted to slip out. I do love cats, but the apron was hideous. I mean, it would be all right for five-year-olds playing dress-up, but I couldn't see anyone else ever wearing it. The cats were fluorescent colors, and neon-green lace lined the bottom and went around the pocket.

"You hate it, don't you?"

"No!" I lied. "You know I love cats. That was really thoughtful of you. I'm going to wear it tomorrow."

He smiled. "I picked out the material and had my mom sew it. She said the colors might be a little intense."

My heart melted. I tried not to read anything into it. He was probably trying to make sure I kept giving him free cookies.

"Your mom sews? That's neat. Not many people do anymore."

"Yeah, she's pretty good. I didn't appreciate it when I was growing up. She always made my clothes, and it was so embarrassing. She didn't do it to save money. She did it because she thought it was fun."

"Have your parents ever come to the diner?"

"Not in a long time. They farm, so they're ten minutes out of town and don't like to drive much. I'll bring them in sometime. They usually come around for all the harvest fun."

"Harvest fun?"

"Muddy Creek isn't the most popular place on the map, but when October comes, we get a lot of traffic. There's a big festival each week before Halloween with lots of food trucks and fun things for kids. Bouncy houses and pony rides. That kind of thing. There is a massive corn maze. The town makes more money in October than the rest of the year combined. People come from far away."

"That sounds fun."

"You might want to consider closing on the days of the festival. You would probably make a lot of money, but you would miss everything. People can eat at the food trucks. You could get a booth and sell cookies or something."

I rubbed my dry lips together. "I'll have to think about it."

"At least go to the corn maze. It's epic. Two farmers do it together, and it goes for over two miles."

I shook my head in amazement. "That's huge! With my luck, I'd never find my way out."

"They have a lot of people looking for stragglers."

"I've never been to a corn maze."

"Then you really need to go. It's open all October. There are hayrides too."

I smiled. "I can't picture you going through a corn maze or on a hayride."

He shrugged. "I don't do it anymore. Ever since I've been sheriff, I've been on duty. The teen population always likes to do a lot of pranks. We bring in extra officers for the festival because there's trouble every year. It's usually harmless, but it's still a problem."

"It's too bad you don't get to enjoy it."

"I still have fun. I patrol around the booths and eat enough to make myself sick."

I grinned. "I can't believe you're in such good shape with the amount of food you pack in." My smile faded, and I felt the temperature rise in my face. I couldn't believe I'd just complimented and insulted him at the same time. "I mean... not that you eat too much, it's..."

He laughed as my sentence faded away. "I tend to eat too much when there's a celebration or when I come in here. I've had to up my workout schedule since you started baking. So are you going to make time for the festival?"

"I might. If most people will be eating at food trucks, it's probably a waste for me to stay open."

"You won't regret it. I've always liked the fall festivals better than Christmas. Even the grumpy part of the population seems to enjoy it. And if you think I can pack it away, you should see Boyd. He's always sick for a day or two after."

It had been a long time since I'd done anything fun. I mean, I did small things, but never anything noteworthy. Most of my friends from high school and college had gotten married, and even though I'd met new people, they were never the type I spent a lot of time with. My friends here were all in a different stage of life than me, and I wasn't sure if they would want to run through corn mazes. Still, it sounded fun. And what harm could come from closing down the diner for a day?

Chapter 4

The noise in the diner was the loudest I'd ever heard. No complaining here. Noise meant business. We had placed a sign outside offering a free cinnamon roll with breakfast. I wasn't sure if that was the reason for the breakfast crowd, but it was my best guess. José and Darcy had things taken care of in the kitchen, but the servers were overwhelmed since we were short of help during school hours. I donned my hideous cat apron and went out to help. I'd taken extra care with my hair today, curling it and hoping it would take attention away from the neon apron.

When I mentioned wanting to repair the broken jukebox to José, he'd tried fixing it after hours. I didn't want him to be overworked, but he said he enjoyed trying to fix things. He'd been a mechanic before he worked here. So far, he hadn't had any success, but he hadn't given up. For now, we were using the diner's sound system to play Elvis Presley in the background. That had been Barbra's idea. She loved the king.

I placed a plate of scrambled eggs and bacon in front of one customer and asked if he needed anything. He was a tall man with sandy brown hair, broad shoulders, and eyes that wouldn't meet mine. When he answered, it was almost inaudible in the noisy diner. He shook his head and dug into his eggs, his eyes going to the window. I could tell when I wasn't needed, so I hurried away to pick up another order.

I picked up a tray with three plates on it and read the small note José left telling me which table it went to. Before I could deliver it, José came out of the kitchen and stood close to me. I raised my brow in question.

He leaned even closer. "That man you just served is Karl Lattmire," he whispered.

"Who?"

"He's the man who used to carpool with Patrick."

"Ohhhhh. Thanks." My mind wasn't on Darcy's husband but the crazy morning crowd. I served table two and tried to come up with a reason to speak with Karl. He obviously wasn't looking for conversation, and talking to people I didn't know wasn't my favorite thing to do. I forced myself, and I was getting better, but talking to a stranger about a possible murder was almost beyond me.

I served the next few customers and wiped off an empty table. If we could keep crowds like this, we would have to consider hiring more people, and fast. The crowd must have peaked because the bell hadn't tinkled in over five minutes. I wiped a barstool and realized I was procrastinating. Karl was almost finished with his food.

The serving shelf was lined with cinnamon rolls on small plates. I grabbed one and took it over to Karl. I placed it in front of him and smiled.

He frowned down at the pastry. "I don't normally eat dessert at breakfast time. It slows down the metabolism."

I kept my smile and said nothing about the massive plate of bacon he'd just consumed. "I can give it to you to go if you want. They're better fresh, though." I slid into the seat across from him before I could chicken out. His frown went even deeper, but I couldn't miss this opportunity.

"I'm sorry to bother you, Mr. Lattmire."

He raised his brow. "Do I know you?"

"Sorry, no. My name is Ivy Clark. I own the diner."

He nodded but didn't say anything.

"I'm sorry to pry, but would it be okay if I asked you some questions about Patrick Henderson?"

His eyes narrowed, and he crossed his arms. "I don't like to talk about Patrick. The police questioned me when he first disappeared, and I don't like to think about it."

"I understand, but if there is anything you could tell me, I would appreciate it. I've become friends with Darcy Peterson and would like to help her get closure."

He sighed and ran a hand over his face. "I don't know anything. Patrick wasn't a big talker and neither am I. We drove to work together to save money, but we rarely said more than a sentence to each other."

I nodded. "So you have no ideas or theories about where he might be?"

"No."

"There was nothing suspicious about him?"

He sighed. "Well, there might be one thing. I know he wasn't always at work at the end of the day. Sometimes he came to my car from a different direction, walking with a woman. She always went into his building after he got in the car, so I'm assuming she worked with him. That is the only odd thing about him I can think of."

My heart sped up. This could be something. "Do you remember what she looked like?"

"She stood out to me because she was really thin, like too thin, and she had bright red hair. Not natural red hair, but like bright red. Her lipstick always matched it."

"Did he ever say anything about her?"

"Nope, and I mind my own business." From the tilt of his head, I assumed he was telling me to do the same.

I stood. "Thank you. I'm sorry I bothered you."

He picked up his previously unwanted cinnamon roll and took a bite. His brows rose, and he bit it again. I resisted the urge to smile. It was so fulfilling to see someone appreciate my baking. Especially when they weren't trying to make me feel good about myself.

Livy was watching the dining area and not talking to anyone at the moment, so things were definitely more relaxed. I went into the kitchen to tell José what Karl Lattmire had told me. I stopped as soon as I saw Darcy. I couldn't tell him while she was there. Adding a mysterious woman to everything would only stress her more.

"Do you need help in here?" I asked.

José looked up from the stove. "I think we're doing pretty well. Considering the crowd and all, I think we're keeping up."

Darcy nodded from over by a large carton of eggs. "I think we're good. I wouldn't say no to another cook, but we're managing."

"I'm going to put ads up for bussers, a cook or two, and maybe another daytime server."

"That's a good idea," Darcy said, not looking up from her work. "You should ask Brian Hooper if you can put ads in the library. He has a big bulletin board for stuff like that. There isn't a lot to do in town, so the teenagers like to hang out there."

I smiled. "That's a good idea. Thanks."

The diner stayed busy for the entire day. There were slower times, but it was never empty like I'd seen it when Linda was the owner. I rotated between helping in the kitchen and serving. I'd never seen myself as a business owner, but it agreed with me. Being busy and small-town country life was growing on me. I still missed Arizona, but I could tell this was where I would stay.

At the end of the day, I handed out paychecks and watched everyone leave. Everyone except José.

"So," he said, startling me from my thoughts. "What did Karl have to say? I could tell you were thinking about it all day."

"He didn't say much, but I have a feeling it might have been relevant." I told him about the conversation I had with Karl. José's mouth turned down as I spoke.

He rubbed his chin. "Patrick wasn't a philanderer. I'm almost sure of it."

"But could you really be sure? I mean, it sounds suspicious to me."

"I guess there are always people who surprise you, and it would surprise me. So what is the next step?"

"I'm thinking of going to the city and finding where he worked. I'll see if there is someone who matches the description Karl gave me."

José leaned against the wall and folded his arms. "I'm pretty sure it was a big office building. I don't think they're going to let you go in and look at everyone. How would you even ask to do that?"

"I'll park outside and watch. I can check their hours, so I'll only have to be there for a short time."

"Okay, but it's been five years. The woman might not work there anymore."

"I know, but I don't have a better idea. If she isn't there, I'll ask someone."

He grinned. "You'll ask if they know a really thin woman with fake red hair?"

I laughed. "Maybe." I grabbed my phone from my pocket and sent Darcy a text, asking her what the company Patrick worked for was called. Then I would search for the hours and address. I really hoped this would lead me to better clues than I had.

"Texting Darcy?"

"Yes." I took off the cat apron and tossed it in the laundry basket. I'd worn it all day and hadn't even seen Jett. There was no way I would have worn it if I'd known he wouldn't be in. I wasn't the type of person who could wear the same apron for more than a day without washing it. I was always covered in flour and who knows what else. There had to be a way to let Jet see me in the apron and then for it to accidentally rip or burn up.

"Did you make the apron?" José asked, pointing at the laundry.

"No, it was a gift."

"It's very... bright. It will help you stay visible if the power goes out."

I laughed. "It's pretty bad."

"Who made it? Barbra? She's sewn some interesting things in her day."

"No, it was...uh, Mrs. Malone." I told my face to stay passive, but I was sure I looked guilty.

"Mrs. Malone? Jett's mom?" José slapped his leg and laughed. "No wonder you wore it. I thought it went against your usual look."

I shook my head and sighed with relief when my phone chimed. I pushed in my password, and my eyes scanned the text. "Patrick worked at Trenton Communications, Inc. She sent the address. They open at eight. Ugh. I hoped it was earlier. If the diner is packed like today, you'll need me."

His eyes sparkled. "I doubt it will be. Tuesday is always the slowest day. You go, and we'll manage. I wish I could go with you. I've never done a stakeout."

"It's hardly a stakeout."

"Are you taking binoculars?"

I grinned. "No. I'm not hiding. I'll be sitting in plain sight."

"That's no fun. It will be more tolerable knowing you aren't having fun while I'm slaving away here."

I just smiled and shook my head. "If it comes to doing an actual stakeout, I'll close the diner."

"Take Boyd. He'll be upset if you don't."

"Good idea. I'll go talk to him before I turn in."

"Did you see his new wheels?"

"No. I thought Boyd didn't drive?"

He chuckled. "He doesn't like to. It's not a car."

Now, I was intrigued. "What is it?"

"Go talk to him and ask."

After saying goodbye to José and checking on Creepers, I drove to Boyd's house. His house was a cute two-story with a large wraparound porch and old-fashioned shutters. He'd lived there his entire life, and he kept it in good shape in memory of his parents. He'd told me he was even born there.

As soon as I stepped out of my gray Kia Soul, Boyd came out and waved. I climbed the three steps and met him on the porch.

"Ivy, how are things? I was going to come for lunch today, but I rode by, and it was much too crowded."

"Rode by?"

A smile covered his entire face. "Yep. Everyone is going to see a lot more of me in town. I got myself a bike."

"Oh? That's awesome."

"More than awesome. I got me one of those bikes with electricity or something like that. Those things really buzz. It's the most fun I've had since we solved Rob's murder. You'll have to take it for a spin."

The image of Boyd flying by on an electric bike made me smile. "I hope you wear a helmet."

"Of course I do. I'll let you take it for a spin anytime you want."

I laughed. "Thanks."

"When I noticed the diner was busy, I went home and tried to find a recipe online. Barbra keeps telling me I should cook more. Have you ever found a recipe on the internet?"

"Lots of times."

He shook his head. "I had the hardest time. I wanted a recipe for a casserole, and when I clicked on it, the woman who wrote it told a story about her dog. Apparently, her dog inspired her to cook more. Then, she told a story about growing up in southern Idaho. It took me ten minutes to find the recipe!"

"There's usually a button at the top to let you go straight to the recipe."

"I just don't get why she had to talk about her entire life first. I wanted to make the casserole, not hear about her eighth-grade piano recital."

I giggled. "People like to give their backstories."

"Well, it was exhausting to get through. Sorry for distracting you. What brings you out here?"

"I'm going to go watch the building Patrick used to work at. Karl Lattmire told me Patrick used to go somewhere with a woman who worked there, and I want to talk to her. It's probably nothing, but I want to make sure. Do you want to join me tomorrow?"

His eyes danced. "Course I do. Are you going to drive, or should we take my bike?"

"That would be a pretty long bike ride. I'll pick you up in the morning."

"Sounds good. Does Jett know?"

"No. I haven't seen him today."

"Better to ask forgiveness than permission, anyway."

I tilted my head and folded my arms. "We aren't doing anything he could disapprove of. All we're doing is watching. Well, unless we find the woman, then we might try to talk to her."

Boyd laughed. "I'll be ready."

Chapter 5

B oyd and I sat in my car and watched people enter the five-story communications building. Boyd had insisted on stopping and getting sub sandwiches and soda because he said that was what you should do in a stakeout, even if it was early in the morning. He had also brought binoculars, and he was wearing dark glasses that I imagined made looking through binoculars difficult. I took a picture of him sipping his soda and watching through the binoculars and sent it to José.

I hoped the woman stood out because a lot of people were walking around in business casual. It would be hard to pick out a person we didn't know. My eyes were only searching for red hair. With luck, the woman still liked that color and was still employed here.

"Look, there," he said, pointing. I followed his finger and saw a middle-aged woman with the reddest hair and lipstick I had ever seen. She wore a bright yellow dress with a green belt and ankle boots. Her purse looked like an eight-year-old girl with a love for bling had attacked it. Her entire look would cause anyone to stare in confusion.

I took a deep breath. "That must be her. Now what?"

"She's at least fifty. I don't see Patrick running around with someone like that. You go talk to her, and I'll keep watch. Hurry before she goes in."

I hopped out of the car and walked swiftly toward her. "Excuse me?"

She stopped and looked at her watch. "I don't have any cash on me, hon," she said with a Southern twang.

I blinked. Did I really look like I was asking for a hand-out? "My name is Ivy. Can I talk to you for a minute? It's about Patrick Henderson."

The woman's shoulders slumped. "Are you with the police? I thought they decided he'd run off."

"No, I'm just a friend of the family."

She looked at her watch again. "Oh, well, I don't see what help I can be."

I didn't have time to beat around the bush. "I heard you used to hang out with Patrick outside work. Is that true?"

She barked out a short laugh. "Hang out with Patrick? That's hilarious. Hey, Marv?" she said to a man walking past. "Tell the boss man I'll be a little late. I'm answering some questions about Patrick."

"Sure thing," the man said over his shoulder as he passed.

"Thanks, love." She turned back to me. "I never spent time outside work with Patrick. He was a nice guy, but a little dull. The only place I ever went to with him was the bank."

My mouth turned down. "The bank?"

"Once a week, two employees take all the money to the bank. They send two to keep everyone honest, I guess. We walk over because it's just around the corner."

"I see. Is there anything you can tell me about Patrick? Anything that might help me find him?"

She patted my arm. "I hate to say it, hon, but I bet he's dead."

"Why?"

"Patrick was a good guy. Helpful, compassionate. He wouldn't run out on people. Everyone he worked with agrees."

I nodded. "So he didn't have any enemies that you know of?"

"No. He was a likable enough guy, and he avoided confrontation. He even brought treats to work once a week. He seemed distracted toward the end. There were times he was late, and he seemed down. I didn't ask him about it because we didn't have that kind of relationship."

"How long was he like that?"

Her mouth turned down. "It's been a long time. I don't remember exactly. It had to have been over a week because it stood out to me as being odd. Everyone has a bad day, but he was having a bad month or two."

"Thank you. If you think of anything else, could you call me?"

"Sure. My name is Marla, by the way."

I pulled a small notepad from my pocket and wrote my name and number on it. I tore it out and handed it to her.

She glanced down at it. "Are you from Muddy Creek?"

"I moved there recently."

"Did you know Patrick?"

"No. I know his wife."

She pursed her lips. "That poor thing. It's too bad she can't get any closure. I suppose that is what you are trying to do?"

"I hope to."

"Well, good luck to you, honey. I'm rooting for you."

"Thank you."

I went back to the car and told Boyd everything. "I think this was a dead end."

"Maybe, maybe not," Boyd said. "Knowing he was having a terrible month could be helpful."

"You're right. It means something might have led up to his disappearance. He might have been involved in something shady."

He wrinkled his nose. "He didn't seem the sort."

"We know Darcy's mom has money issues. What if he did as well? He could have been doing something to try to help his family and made some bad choices."

"I suppose. What next?"

I turned on the car. "I guess we go home. They might need me in the diner today." We pulled out and drove toward Muddy Creek. "Patrick didn't have enemies, and people liked him. I'm surprised his car never turned up."

"Word on the street is that Patrick has a brother in the slammer. Could he be involved?"

I chewed on the inside of my cheek and thought. "I don't think so. Darcy said he's in jail. She's never even met him. I guess we could talk to their parents. I wanted to avoid that, if possible, because I doubt they want to be reminded of it."

Trying to focus on the road and not space out while driving was hard to do when you were on a small road with no other cars, and the flat Kansas prairie was the only scenery. Marla didn't have any reason to lie. I thought Patrick might be in a relationship with her, but when I met her, I changed my mind. She was at least fifteen years older than he was, and her story made sense.

I still wanted to speak with Matt Hooper. From everything I'd heard, he didn't spend much time in Muddy Creek. He had a house, though, so he hadn't lost his connection to the town. I needed to talk to Brian about leaving ads in the library, so I might as well ask him more about his brother as well.

I would have to wait until a slow moment or after closing. The library closed at the same time as the diner, though, and I didn't know where Brian lived. I smiled when I pictured myself putting Creepers outside and waiting to see if he would lead me to Brian. That would be expecting a lot. Whenever I put Creepers outside, he meowed to go back inside.

Boyd cleared his throat. "You are either thinking about the case or Sheriff Malone's pretty blue eyes. From the smile, I would guess the second."

I gave Boyd my best side-eye glare. "I was thinking about the case, and Jett's eyes are brown. Haven't you known him forever?"

He chuckled. "I sure do. And I knew his eyes were brown. I just wondered if you did."

I kept my eyes on the road and shook my head. I wasn't giving anything else away. "Do you know where Matt Hooper's house is?"

"Sure do. I know where everyone in and around Muddy Creek lives."

"Do you want to go over and see if he's there later today?"

"Why?"

"If Darcy dated Matt, and he never got over it, he could be a suspect."

"It wouldn't take much to convince me. I've never been a fan of Matt Hooper. In my opinion, he has always been bigheaded, moody, and the opposite of Brian. Brian would give you the shirt off his back. Matt is more likely to tell everyone your shirt is ugly and then steal it, anyway."

I tapped my fingers against the steering wheel. "Has he stolen things?"

"Nah, that was probably unfair of me to say. He just rubs me the wrong way."

"Do you know why he and Darcy broke up?"

"Nope. I'm guessing she wouldn't mind if you ask her since she's the one who asked you to look into all this. Are you leaning toward Matt being the murderer?"

I turned up the air-conditioning. It was getting cool outside, but the sun beat against the car. "No. I've never met Matt, and we don't even know if there was a murder. In my mind, it makes sense to at least look into Matt. Everyone I've heard of who knew Patrick thought he was a nice guy. It sounds like Matt spread rumors about him and is the only person so far who didn't like him."

We rode in silence for the rest of the trip. Boyd had me take him to the diner so he could eat. I couldn't imagine how hungry he could be after we ate the huge subs. I think Boyd liked to hang out at the diner so he could talk to everyone and not be home alone.

People were at the diner, but not as many as the day before. The servers had everything under control, so I went into the kitchen. Creepers sat under José's stool, and José and Darcy were busy frying something. Darcy's daughter, Netty, sat on the floor poking at my cat.

"People are going to freak out if they see a cat in the kitchen," I said, squatting down and pulling Creepers toward me. "I don't know how he got out."

José turned and looked at me. "I doubt anyone would care. They would rather see a cat than mice. Everyone around here has cats. It just makes sense."

I cuddled Creepers against me and went closer to Darcy. The cat protested, and I put him down. "Hey, Darcy? Do you mind if I ask you a personal question?"

She raised her brow. "Go ahead."

"Why did you and Matt Hooper break up?"

She laughed. "I didn't expect that question. It was so long ago. I started dating Matt because he was good-looking and popular. As time passed, I realized we had little in common and I didn't enjoy spending time with him. He always wanted to watch basketball, and he would get so angry when his team wasn't winning. He would yell at the TV and throw things. I realized I wasn't happy, so I broke it off."

"And he was upset about it?"

"Yes. He tried to get me to take him back multiple times. He still sends me things every once in a while. I ignore him, but he is persistent."

"And he didn't like Patrick?"

"No." Her eyes jumped to me. "You don't suspect Matt, do you?"

"I'm just trying to piece everything together. I haven't even met him yet. This morning, I met one of Patrick's former coworkers."

"Oh? Anyone I know?"

"Her name was Marla."

Darcy smiled. "I've met Marla. She's a character. Why did you talk to her? She can't be a suspect."

"I'm just gathering information."

"It's really nice of you to do this for me."

"That's what friends are for."

Darcy's eyes teared up, and she turned away. "It's been a while since I had friends."

Netty lay down on the floor, her long brown hair spread against the dark tile. "This is so boring," she said.

"It doesn't look very comfortable down there," I observed.

She glared at me through her neon-green glasses. "I like the floor."

I shrugged and grabbed a mixing bowl. It had been a while since I'd made brownies. I grabbed a hairnet and pulled it over my hair and washed my hands. "Netty, do you want to help me make brownies?"

She glared at me. "Only people I say can call me Netty are allowed."

Darcy turned sharply and put her hands on her hips. "Antonette Peterson! What have I told you about this? Apologize, now."

The girl stared up at the ceiling. "Sorry."

"It's alright," I said, grabbing some sugar from the pantry. "I'll call you Antonette if you wish."

"Antonette was a queen, you know."

"Yep, you told me the day we met." I grabbed some eggs from the fridge.

"I'm going to be just like Marie Antonette when I grow up."

I didn't think now was the time to tell her about the way the queen's life ended. José was smiling to himself. I'd bet he was thinking the same thing.

She pushed herself up onto her elbows. "Can I sit in the diner and have a soda?"

Darcy looked at her and arched her brow.

Netty rolled her eyes. "Please?"

"I suppose," Darcy said. "Go ask Livy very nicely to help you."

She got to her feet. "Alright. I like Livy," she said, giving me a pointed look. She hurried into the dining area, slamming the door behind her.

"Sorry about her," Darcy said. "I think I'm a failure as a mother. She spends too much time with my mom, and she's starting to sound like her."

"She's still young," José said. "The queen will figure things out eventually."

Darcy sighed. "I sure hope so."

Chapter 6

Matt Hooper's house was massive. I'd seen some big houses in Muddy Creek, but none like this. It was a large Victorian home with painted white brick, a steep roof with two turrets, and a wraparound porch. Several large trees dotted the property, and the yard was well cared for.

"He must pay someone to take care of his yard when he's gone," I said as I glanced around.

"I'm sure he does," José said. "The Hoopers have loads of dough."

"He pays the Ericson boys to care for it," Boyd said. "I heard one of them bragging about how much they make."

"There's no garage and no cars, so we can probably look around," I said. "This all feels weird. I don't know what we're looking for."

Boyd scratched his head. "Patrick's bones?"

I shivered. "I doubt it. It's been five years. Even if Matt did it, I doubt any evidence is lying around."

"So why are we here?" he asked.

I shrugged. "I just want to get a feel for everything. I'm going to go look around back. Boyd, do you want to keep watch?"

"Sure."

José followed me to the back. The yard wasn't as big as I imagined, and I could tell where it ended because it went from green-clipped grass to tall weeds. There were no other houses in sight. It was still strange to look out at the flat area. It had a different feeling than the mountains in Arizona. I did like the way the weeds and wildflowers swayed in the breeze. They seemed to go on forever.

I sighed. "I feel like I'm just wandering through this case, hoping something falls into my lap. I hope Darcy isn't disappointed if we can't figure it out."

José stared up at the house. "Don't give up too fast. We have to expect it to take a while. I mean, it all happened so long ago, any evidence might be deeply buried."

I walked along the property, studying the ground. If Matt was hiding anything, he probably had enough money to hide it well. He wouldn't leave it in his backyard.

"Let's go back around front," I said. "I don't see anything."

We rounded the corner, and I couldn't see Boyd. "Where's Boyd?"

José peeked into the car windows. "Not here." We looked down the dirt road, and there was nothing. We hadn't been gone long enough for him to get out of sight.

I looked at the house. "You don't think he went in, do you?"

José moved his jaw from side to side. "I hope not."

"Hey, guys!" Boyd called from above. "I'm here!" We looked up and saw Boyd high in an enormous sycamore tree. My heart dropped into my stomach. That was way too high, and Boyd was no spring chicken.

"What are you doing up there?" I demanded, my hands on my hips. "Are you trying to kill yourself?"

"No, but it would make an amusing story, don't you think?"

José and I shared a look.

"There aren't any window coverings up here. I thought I could look in, but it's too dark."

"Get down here before you fall!" José called.

He chuckled. "Can't. I'm stuck good. Up isn't hard, but down is rough on the knees."

I held my head with my hands and turned to José. "What are we going to do?"

"I can climb up and help him down."

"No, then you will both be stuck up there."

"Not me. I'm in good shape for an old guy."

"I'm fair at climbing, but I don't think I can help him down. I doubt Matt has a ladder. There's no garage or shed to store anything."

"We're going to have to call Jett."

I bit my lower lip. "There has to be another way."

"The fire department has a big ladder."

That also meant involving Jett. Volunteers ran the Muddy Creek fire department, and since there weren't enough, that meant Jett was pretty much in charge of it as well as the law.

"Are you sure you can't climb down?" I asked Boyd.

"Nope. I'm as stuck as a skunk in a pickle jar. But I'm comfy enough, so I can wait."

I moved my lips from side to side and paused when I saw a vehicle coming down the road. A cloud of dust surrounded it, making it hard to identify. When it got closer, I frowned. I recognized Jett's black sheriff's truck.

"There's the sheriff," José said, waving at the truck. "I'm going to text Steve and tell him to bring the fire truck."

I sighed and nodded. Jett was the one I didn't want to find us like this, but it was going to happen, anyway.

He parked the truck on the side of the road and got out, striding toward us. He had on his tan sheriff shirt, dark sunglasses, and a cowboy hat. It reminded me of a gum commercial... or possibly deodorant. Either way, Jett was commercial-worthy. I shook my head and tried to look innocent.

"Hey, all," he said. "I saw you headed this way, and I know there's nothing out here but Matt's house. What are you up to?"

"Just hanging around!" Boyd called from above.

Jett looked up and sighed. "Please tell me Boyd isn't stuck up there."

José laughed. "Oh, he's stuck alright."

Jett crossed his arms and looked at me. I threw my arms into the air. "What? I didn't tell him to climb up there."

"Steve is on his way with the fire truck," José said, looking up from his phone. "He just left."

"You three need to be more careful. What if he falls?"

"I won't fall," Boyd said. "I'm fine up here. Take your time."

Jett rolled his eyes. "You aren't sixty anymore, Boyd. You have to take care."

"If Ivy had kept teaching Zumba, I bet my joints would be better prepared."

I shook my head. I loved teaching Zumba, but with the diner, it was too much. We all stood lost in our own thoughts as we stared up at Boyd.

"Do you want me to sing?" Boyd asked. "Just to pass the time?"

We all ignored him.

Jett gave me a half smile. "I guess I should be glad you and José aren't up there with him."

I smiled back. "We probably would have been if you'd been a few minutes later."

He laughed. "I don't doubt that for a minute."

"So what are the chances of the town not finding out about this?" I asked. "I mean, we don't want Matt to know we were snooping around his house."

"Word travels fast around here. I can tell Steve to keep it quiet, but who knows? What are you all doing here, anyway?"

"We were seeing if Matt was here and looking around."

"Matt isn't around most of the time. I haven't seen him in months. Is he your prime suspect?"

My eyes narrowed. I couldn't see his eyes through his sunglasses, but I was sure they had a mischievous glint. "Are you making fun of us?"

He grinned. "Who me? Nooo! It's normal for the woman who operates the small-town diner to run around with old guys trying to solve crimes."

José crossed his arms. "Who are you calling an old guy?"

"I'm definitely an old guy," Boyd said, "and I'm getting a cramp in my foot."

Jett pointed down the road. "I see a gigantic cloud of dust. I bet that's Steve."

We all watched as the red fire truck came down the dirt road. Everything was so dry, but the sky was overcast, so with luck, it would rain today. The dust clouds a car could kick up when it was dry were impressive. The truck stopped in front of the house, and the man I assumed was Steve got out. He had black hair and wore regular clothes. He walked over to us and looked up.

"Hey, Boyd," he said. "I wish I could say this was the strangest situation I've ever gotten you out of."

"Hi, Steve," Boyd said. "Let's not talk about any of those other times."

Jett and Steve got Boyd down with little trouble, while José and I sat on the front porch.

As soon as Boyd stepped off the ladder, he grabbed his leg and stretched. "That was an adventure."

Jett turned to him and put a hand on his shoulder. "Let's not do that again, alright?"

Boyd chuckled. "Not unless it's necessary. Hey, Steve, do I get to ride on the fire truck?"

Steve laughed. "That's fine by me. Do you want to come too, José?"

"Why not? I've never been on a fire truck before." The three of them loaded into the truck and drove off.

Jett turned to me. "Try not to let Boyd climb trees."

I threw my hands up. "I didn't. José and I were behind the house when he did it. I never would have let him."

Jett touched his cheek. "I felt rain. It's about time. This has been a dry year. Before we know it, we'll get snow, then I'll be complaining about that."

"It's pretty overcast. What's with the sunglasses?"

He took them off, and I cringed. He had a black eye. "Just hiding my embarrassment."

"Ouch. Fight? I bet the other guy looks worse."

"Breaking up a fight, and I think I'm the only one with a mark. Word to the wise: avoid bingo night at the library. Those old ladies are brutal."

I laughed. "That makes two times you've been punched in the face in the few months I've known you."

He grinned. "Hey, it's not an average or anything. Those are the only two times I've ever been punched in the face in my life."

I felt the rain on my arm and face.

He frowned. "We better get going. We don't want to be stuck on a dirt road if it starts pouring. I've gotten stuck before, and it took hours to get the truck out the next day."

Chapter 7

I pulled up to the diner and breathed a sigh of relief. As soon as I left Matt's house, the heavens opened and dumped buckets of water on my windshield. I had never seen rain like that in my life. I stared out at the rain and tried to will myself to run inside. A garage would be a really nice thing right about now.

Grabbing my purse, I bolted outside and ran the ten feet to the door. I fumbled with the keys and let myself in. I was wet even though I'd only been out for a few seconds. Shivering, I made my way up to my room. I grabbed my key, and when I went to put it in the lock, the door creaked open.

Fear ran down my spine as I peeked into my dark room. The window was open, and rain streamed onto the window seat. I could believe I'd accidentally left my room unlocked, but I'd never opened my window. Searching the room sounded like a stupid idea. If someone was there, what was I going to do? Part of me wanted to run back into the storm, but I needed to find Creepers.

Pulling my phone from my pocket, I quickly texted Jett. I wasn't sure what to say, so I just said that someone had been in my room and might still be there. I was almost sure no one was there, but I felt a panic I hadn't had since watching scary movies as a kid.

"Creepers?" I whispered. There was no answer. "Creepers?" I pulled a small can of pepper spray from my purse and flipped on the light. I closed the window and walked over to my wardrobe. That was the most obvious place to hide. Holding up the pepper spray, I threw open the door. Nothing. I got down on my hands and knees and slowly moved the bedspread. Nothing but a cat toy. The bathroom was clear as well. If anyone was still here, then they were in the diner because there was nowhere else to hide.

Where was Creepers? My eyes flew over the room and stopped on a piece of paper lying on my bed. I rushed over and picked it up. In bold Sharpie, it said "Mind your business." I crumpled the paper and ran downstairs, flipping on all the lights.

"Creepers," I called. "Creepers!" I looked under all the tables and in the kitchen. He usually made noise if I called him. Bursting through the door, I ran outside. The rain pelted me, but I didn't care. "Creepers!" I yelled. The storm was so loud that I barely heard my own voice. Lights from a vehicle bounced across the diner and stopped next to my car.

Jett stepped out of his truck and grabbed my arm. "Are you okay?"

"Yes, but I can't find Creepers!"

He guided me back inside, and I barely noticed the puddle that blew into the diner.

"I have to find him," I said.

He shook his head. "The storm is too bad. If he's out there, he's going to be hiding. You'll never find him."

"I have to try."

A meow came from the window. Creepers peered out at us from behind the blinds. I hurried over and pulled him out. "What do you think you're doing?" I asked, cuddling him close. He clawed at me, not enjoying my cold, wet hug. I kissed his head and put him down.

"He didn't answer when I called him."

"I'll search and see if anyone's here."

"No one's here. I checked."

"That's not the best idea. If you think someone might be hiding somewhere, you should leave and wait for help."

"I know, but I had to find Creepers. I found a note on my bed." The crumpled paper was on the floor. I picked it up and handed it to Jett.

His eyes scanned it. "You have to stop looking for Patrick. It's too dangerous."

"But now we know something is up," I protested as I tried to control the chatter of my teeth. "If Patrick left of his own free will, why would someone do this?"

"You're right. I'm going to reopen the case. You need to stay out of it."

I clenched my jaw and kept my reply to myself. "Not many people know I'm looking into this. I've only talked to Karl and Marla. That means it's probably one of them."

Jett crossed his arms and shivered. "It's possible, but it's also likely someone overheard you. You talked to Karl in the diner when it was full of people."

He was right. I needed to be more discreet. "I suppose it's also possible that José or Boyd told someone. Come into the kitchen, and I'll make some hot chocolate."

We went into the kitchen, and Jett searched the room. I poured water and chocolate powder into the hot chocolate machine and flipped it on.

"I'm going to make sure we locked the front door, then I'll search the rest of the diner."

"Alright." I wanted to change my clothes, but it seemed rude since Jett was stuck in wet clothes and it was my fault. Creepers ran through the kitchen, chasing invisible lint. He always got hyper before bedtime.

There were no mirrors in the kitchen, which saved me from knowing just how bad I looked. I pushed my fingers through my hair so it wouldn't be matted to my face and put on some ChapStick.

Jett came back in and looked at me. "The lock to your bedroom is pathetic. Someone could pop it with a credit card."

"I know. I need to replace it."

"I'll come do it tomorrow."

I grabbed two mugs and filled them with hot chocolate. "You don't need to do that. I can replace a doorknob." I handed him a mug.

"Thanks." He took a sip. "I don't think anyone broke into the diner. The front door doesn't look like it's been bothered. My guess is that someone slipped up there when the diner was open."

"I should get security cameras."

He nodded. "Tomorrow we can ask all the employees if they saw Karl or Matt in here."

"Matt wouldn't know I've been snooping. He doesn't even know me."

"Word gets around pretty fast. If anyone overheard you or suspects you were looking into it, everyone could know by now."

I sipped the hot chocolate and sank down on a stool. It had been a long day, and I was ready to be dry and in bed.

"I'm going to stay in the diner tonight," Jett said. "Tomorrow, I'll go to Hal's to get a better lock and see if he carries cameras or alarm systems."

I yawned. "You can't stay here. You're soaked."

"There's always a spare pair of clothing in my truck."

"You don't need to stay. The note wasn't exactly a threat."

"Someone popped your lock to leave that. I count that as a threat. Why don't you go to bed? I'll grab my stuff and keep watch."

"Alright." I was too tired to argue. "Come on, Creepers." I took my hot chocolate and Creepers up the stairs and placed the cat on the bed. I looked at the wet window seat and sighed. The carpet was wet as well. I grabbed a towel and wiped it the best I could. The carpet would have to dry itself.

I fed Creepers and took a quick shower. I dressed in my warm pajamas and crawled into bed. Creepers climbed on top of me, and that was the last thing I remembered. I don't even remember dreaming.

The following morning, I slept in. The smell of breakfast made my stomach growl. I hurried to get dressed and pulled my hair into a ponytail. I'd taken a shower the night before, so it would have to count for today. When I entered the diner, people sat at four tables. My eyes widened when I spotted Jett sleeping in one of the booths. He was propped against the wall with his legs on the bench. He was going to be stiff when he woke up. I couldn't believe the noise from the diner didn't wake him.

I went into the kitchen and grabbed an apron. "Hey, sorry I'm late. I slept in."

José and Darcy both looked up from their work. José tilted his head. "What happened after we left last night? When we came in this morning, Jett was sleeping in a booth."

"Someone broke into my room and left me a note."

Darcy gasped. "What did it say?"

"Mind your business." I cringed when Darcy's eyes narrowed. It sounded like I'd insulted her. "That's what the note said. Whoever did it left my window open, so things got wet, and I couldn't find Creepers. Jett came over to make sure everything was safe, and we stayed up too late. I should have set an alarm."

"No, don't worry about it," José said. "We're getting a smooth system going on here."

"I wanted to get up early this morning to decorate for the season. Halloween decorations are my favorite. I don't have any, so I'll have to find some."

"I can paint some things on the window," Darcy offered. "I'm really good at it. Maybe some pumpkins or cute ghosts would look nice."

"That would be great. Thanks."

"I wonder if I should wake up Jett and tell him to go home and get some good sleep. He's going to have a terrible kink in his neck. I bet he tried to stay up all night."

José grinned. "Then what will all the customers stare at?"

"That's probably another good reason to get him to leave. Everyone will wonder what's going on."

Darcy sighed. "I shouldn't have asked you to help me. I don't want anyone getting hurt."

"In a way, it's a good thing," I said. "Now we know that something happened. Jett is reopening the case."

Her eyes widened. "Really?"

"Yep. I'm going to go wake him."

I went into the dining area and tried to think of the best way to wake him. The last thing I needed was to draw the attention of the customers. I went up close and grabbed his boot, moving it around a little. His snore caused me to jump. The couple at the table next to him and Sarah and Livy all laughed.

"He's really out," I said.

"About once every five minutes, he snores like that," Livy said. "We weren't sure if we should wake him or not. It looks like he got into a fight or something."

I smiled when I thought about bingo night.

"Sheriff Malone?" I said, moving his foot again. He was too far back for me to shake his shoulder. "Jett? Jett?"

"Just whap him with a newspaper," Barbra said from one booth. Her hair was light blue today.

I shook his foot more vigorously. "Jett! Wake up!" There was no use in being quiet. Everyone in the diner was already watching, and they all looked amused. His head fell farther to the side, then bounced back up, but he still didn't wake. "I guess I can leave him here. It doesn't look like we need the table."

"We should video him," Barbra said, pulling out her phone. "It's always good to have a little blackmail."

"Leave the poor man alone," Barbra's friend Opal said. "He probably deserves a good sleep more than any other person in this town."

I thought again of how sore his neck was going to be. I put one hand on the table to support my weight and leaned over to shake his arm. I grabbed his sleeve and moved it back and forth. "Jett!"

"Hmm?" he muttered.

"You need to wake up."

"Okay."

I waited. His eyes didn't open.

"Jett?" I shook his arm again, but he didn't respond. "Fine. Stay here and let Barbra take pictures of you."

"Huh?" he said, sliding down. His legs went off the edge of the bench and bumped into mine. I lost my footing and fell right onto him. My elbow caught him in the stomach.

"Oof!" His eyes opened wide. I pushed up on his arms, trying to get up. "Ivy? What's going on?"

My hand slipped, so instead of getting up, I fell under the table. My elbow hit the hard tile floor, and I cringed. I watched Jett's legs as he sat up. A moment later, he glanced under the table.

"What are you doing?" he asked.

I got onto my hands and knees and crawled backward until I could stand. Ignoring all the giggles from the patrons and probably the servers wasn't easy. "I was trying to wake you up!"

He stood and rubbed his stomach. "By body-slamming me?"

"I slipped."

Barbra held up her camera. "And I got it all on video! It's going viral for sure!"

My face was already cherry red. "Don't post that anywhere!"

"Send it to me," Jett said, winking at Barbra.

I put my hands on my waist. "Delete it!"

The door opened, and Marla came in. She wore a bright purple dress and clogs. Her eyes scanned the room until they landed on me. "Hello, Ivy. I tried texting you, but it wasn't going through. Something happened yesterday that I thought you might want to know about."

I hurried over to her, ignoring my throbbing elbow. "Oh?"

"Yesterday evening, I saw Patrick Henderson."

Chapter 8

Jett came striding across the room. "You saw Patrick Henderson? Where? Did you speak to him?"

Marla glanced at the star on Jett's shirt. "Hello, Sheriff. Yep, I saw Patrick walking down the main street, just as happy as you please. He was holding a Starbucks cup and talking to someone. I didn't speak with him because I lost sight of him when I waited for a traffic light."

I realized my mouth was open, so I closed it. "Are you sure it was him?"

"Positive. He was probably thirty pounds heavier, but it has been five years. When I couldn't get ahold of you, I hurried on over to tell y'all in person."

"How did you find me?"

"I just asked someone on the street, and they pointed me in this direction. Mind if I have some breakfast?"

"Of course you can," I said, leading her to a booth. Jett followed us.

Marla looked up at him. "No need to follow me, darlin'. I can't answer any more questions because that was all I saw."

Jett tilted his head. "Did you see who he was with?"

"Nope, sorry. I was so shocked at seeing him that I didn't even think about the other person."

"Well, thank you for the information." Jett turned and disappeared into the kitchen.

"Sarah?" I said, getting the woman's attention. "This is my friend Marla. Give her what she wants. It's on the house."

Sarah smiled. "Sure thing."

Marla grinned. "That's nice of you."

"I owe you. You did us a favor by coming all the way out here."

"And I'll come again or call you if I ever see him again."

I rushed to the kitchen, curious about what Jett would tell Darcy. When I entered, he was leaning against the counter, eating something while Darcy and José cooked.

My eyes went from Jett to Darcy, then back to Jett. He shook his head slightly, so I didn't say anything. He walked casually out the back door, and I followed. I closed the door gently behind me.

It was chilly and wet, so I crossed my arms. "What do you think?"

"I'm not sure. I feel a bit conflicted about her story."

I rubbed my arms. "What do you mean?"

"She could be telling the truth, or she could be lying to get you to stop looking for Patrick."

"Why would she do that?"

He rubbed his chin. "Well, what if she's guilty? If she did something to Patrick, she probably thought she was home free after all these years. Then you come along asking questions. What does she do? Pretend she saw him."

"Then people might not search because it would mean he left on his own."

"Exactly."

"Is that what you think happened?"

"No, but it's a possibility. It's also possible she came yesterday and broke into your room."

I looked out at the muddy world and sighed. "If she's telling the truth, then what? If Patrick is out there somewhere living his life, that will break Darcy's heart."

"But at least she would know and have closure."

"Do we tell her what Marla said?"

"I'm not sure. Not yet. I need to think about it." He rubbed his eyes. "I'm so tired that I can't even focus."

"I should have let you sleep."

He grinned. "I probably needed an elbow to the stomach. I'm not sure anything else would have woken me up."

"Your eye looks a lot better this morning. It's turning yellow."

"Well, that's something."

"Are you allowed to work your own hours? You should go home and take a nap."

"I'll just go eat breakfast, and that should get me going."

"Go sit, and I'll send out some food."

I returned to the diner and peeked through the window at Marla. She was sipping something and staring at her phone. I was pretty sure I believed her, but I had only talked to her briefly. And what were the chances Patrick just showed up right after I started looking for him?

Why would Patrick disappear for five years and then turn up in the city, walking around and drinking Starbucks? If he had been held somewhere against his will, wouldn't he contact Darcy? I wanted to drop everything, drive to the city, and look for him, but the chances of finding him around that many people were slim.

After I had breakfast sent out to Jett, I walked to the county store to see if they had any Halloween decorations. I found some window paint for Darcy and pumpkin lights to put around the inside of the diner. There were some cute ghosts I could hang from the lights. For being a small store, they had an impressive selection of decorations. By the time I left, my wallet was lighter.

The library was on my way home, so I stopped to talk to Brian. He was in the children's area, reading a book to a bunch of toddlers. I stood and watched for a moment. Brian was pretty good at doing voices. I found the bulletin board with the fliers hanging on it. A lot of them advertised different booths that would be at the festival.

"You must be Ivy Clark," someone said from behind me. I spun around to see a tall man who resembled Brian. This had to be Matt.

I put on my friendliest smile. "I'm Ivy."

He held out his hand, and I shook it. "Matt Hooper. Nice to meet you."

"You too. I'm a big fan of Brian's."

He nodded. "Everyone is. I've been meaning to speak to you. Can we talk in the auditorium?"

"There's an auditorium?"

He rolled his eyes. "Brian calls it an auditorium. It's small, but I guess it works for Muddy Creek." He led me over to a door and pulled it open. I was a little nervous. What could he possibly want to talk to me about? If he was the one who broke into the diner, I shouldn't be going with him when no one knew I was here.

I pulled out my phone and texted Jett. "Just let me tell my friend I'm talking to you. I don't want him to worry when I'm late," I lied. I figured I was safe now. Matt knew that someone knew I was with him. That made me feel better. I followed him into a room the size of a school classroom. There were three rows of ten chairs facing a baby grand piano.

"Nice," I said. "Who uses the piano?"

"Brian hopes people will reserve it someday to have a recital. I don't think anyone has. I think the only thing anyone reserves it for is bingo night."

I turned to him and tried my best not to appear nervous. "What did you want to talk to me about?"

"Patrick."

I nodded. "What about him?"

He cocked his head and studied me. "I know you're looking for him."

I took a step back. "Yeah, but I'm not sure I'm getting anywhere."

"I had nothing to do with it."

I raised my brow. "I never said you did."

"I have security cameras at my house."

Heat crept up my neck, and I'm sure I was bright red. "Oh."

He smiled. "You don't have to be embarrassed. Boyd, on the other hand... he probably should be. I doubt he is, though." We both laughed.

"I wish I had a camera pointing up in the tree," he said. "I had to guess at most of it."

"Sorry," I said. "We shouldn't have been snooping around, but I have to rule out anyone who might have a motive."

His smile faded. "I get that. I was crazy in love with Darcy for a long time. I was even a jerk about Patrick, which he didn't deserve."

"Do you know of anyone else who had something against him?"

"No. I was probably the only one around here. He was generally well-liked."

"You don't have feelings for Darcy anymore?"

"No. It took me a long time, but I came to terms with it and moved on."

"But had you five years ago?"

"No, I can admit that. When Patrick disappeared, I was happy. I thought that might give me a chance, but she made it more than clear it didn't change the way she felt about me. Plus, her kid hates me. She tried to have the sheriff arrest me for standing in front of the aisle she wanted to go down at the store."

I laughed. "That sounds like Antonette."

"She must hate you too if you still have to call her by her queen's name."

"Yes, she tried to have me arrested for sneezing."

"I don't want to point fingers anywhere, but have you grilled Sally Peterson? Darcy's mom tried to stop her wedding."

My eyes widened. Why had no one mentioned that? "She tried to stop it? Why?"

"I don't know. I was on her side at the time, so I wasn't worried about the why. She probably would have acted the same, no matter who the guy was. Sally's a leech, and

Darcy is her only family. Clear back in high school, she made Darcy get a job and give her most of the money."

"Wouldn't it be to her advantage to have Darcy get married, then? Patrick obviously made decent money."

"I think he did, but Darcy moved away, and I'm guessing she stopped giving all her money to her mom. Once he was gone, she had to go back home and become Sally's footstool again. Of course, this all just comes from my speculation."

"Thanks for sharing with me."

"Anytime. I'm not around much, but I like harvest time. I'll stay through the month to attend the festivals."

"I'm excited to see them."

"Muddy Creek throws a great harvest festival. They were so popular we began having them every Saturday of October. The first one is this week."

"Is there one on Halloween?"

"Nope. There isn't one on Halloween because of trick-or-treating."

I thanked Matt and started for the diner. My mind was racing with everything Matt had told me. I'd only met Sally Peterson once, and she hadn't left the best impression on me. Matt seemed like a nice enough guy, but that went against what others had said. I needed to prioritize. Somehow, I needed to figure out whether Patrick was actually alive. Trying to find his murderer would be pointless if he wasn't dead.

Chapter 9

"Boyd, darlin', it doesn't work if you don't follow the rules," Marla said. I smiled as I walked up to a table that held Boyd, Marla, Barbra, and Opal.

"Hi, Marla," I said. "What are you doing here?"

Marla tossed her hair over her shoulder and pointed at a box on the table. "I came to talk to you, but these nice folks invited me to solve a mystery with them."

"Oh?"

Barbra grinned. "We saw these boxes on TV. They send you clues, and you solve the mystery. Since Boyd is so big on mysteries these days, we thought it might be fun."

"Boyd wants to cheat and see all the clues at once," Opal said, glaring at Boyd.

Boyd shrugged. "I just figured it would be easier."

Marla nodded. "Easier, but not more fun."

"I suppose," Boyd said. "You got any cookies today, Ivy?"

I smiled. "That's a silly question. I'll have Livy bring you a few. So what's the game?" I leaned over as Barbra opened the box.

"I already read the rules," Barbra said. "We all get an alias and try to figure out who is guilty of committing a crime." She handed a card to Boyd. "You are Billy Bailey, owner of the hotel and casino. You are forty years old and a bachelor."

Boyd looked down at his card. "That figures. At least my character has hair."

"Marla, you are Silvia Silvester, college professor. You are thirty-eight and married with two dogs and a parakeet."

Boyd snorted. "They aren't very creative, are they?"

Barbra ignored him. "Opal, you are Cara Carpenter, librarian, aged thirty. You have three cats and no relations."

Opal frowned. "Who comes up with these scenarios?"

"I am Holly Hampton, a businesswoman aged thirty. I live in a condo with my husband and kid. Do you wanna play, Ivy?"

I smiled. "No, I have a lot to do. Maybe next time."

"It's the kind of game you can only play once. After you solve it, there really isn't a point in playing again."

"Well, let me know how it goes."

The door opened, and Jett came in.

"Hey, Sheriff!" Barbra called. "Do you want to be Han Hanson? Roof repairman and nighttime custodian?"

Jett's eyebrows came together. "Um...what?" He walked over and looked down at the game.

"Sit down and help us solve a mystery," Marla said.

"I'm on duty."

Opal let out a short laugh. "You're always on duty. Sit down and play. The town won't fall apart if you do something non-sheriffy from time to time."

He pulled a chair over to the end of the table. "Alright, but I'm pretty sure non-sheriffy isn't a word."

"Don't argue with the town librarian," Opal said, grinning.

Jett tilted his head. "You aren't a librarian."

Opal shoved her card at him. "I beg to differ."

This game might get crazy. "José might need me in the kitchen. I'll send out your cookies." I went into the kitchen and piled a plate with treats. Livy grabbed them, and I told her to take them to the eccentric table. She didn't even ask before she took them to Boyd's table.

Ten minutes after the game started, it began to get loud out there. I recognized Marla's and Barbra's laughter. The others were more subtle. I smiled as I mixed some batter. Barbra and Marla had some similarities between them. I hoped it stayed mellow and didn't turn into another bingo night. I peeked out the window to see a large crowd around the table, watching as they played.

Marla threw her head back and laughed at something, and I remembered she'd come here to talk to me. I went over to the table and squeezed my way through the crowd. "Marla, did you need to talk to me?"

Marla looked confused for a moment, and then her eyes went wide. "Sorry, I forgot why I was here." She pulled out her phone and messed with it for a moment. "I saw him again," she said, handing me the phone. I looked down at the picture. It certainly looked like the picture of Patrick. The crowd pushed in to watch the game, and I was pushed back. I sent the picture to my phone and passed Marla's phone back to her.

I went into the kitchen and pulled out my phone. I showed the picture to José. Darla was busy cooking and didn't turn. "Is it Patrick?" I mouthed to him.

He frowned and studied it. "I think so," he whispered, handing it back. I looked at it again. It wasn't an impressive picture. Marla must have zoomed in, so it was a little grainy. I'd have to ask her where she took this before she left.

"Hey, Darcy?"

"Yeah?" she asked without turning.

"Do you think I could go talk to Patrick's parents?"

She froze for a minute. "Why?"

"Just to get their opinions on what might have happened."

She sighed. "I guess so. They aren't the most—receptive people. They are set in their ways and don't enjoy talking about Patrick. I take Netty to see them occasionally, but they don't let me bring him up."

"Because he's gone?"

She looked over her shoulder. "I think so. Patrick was the golden child. Their other son was an embarrassment, so they were happy to brag about Patrick to take people's attention from his brother."

"The police must have questioned them at one point."

"I think they did, but they won't discuss it. It's not surprising. They don't like to talk about a lot of things. It almost kills me to speak to them for more than a few minutes, because they'll only discuss a few subjects."

"What do they like to talk about?"

Darcy frowned. "Let's see. The stock market, farm animals, and movies. Don't talk about movies, though, because they base their opinions of people on what movies they like."

"What type do they like?"

"Anything from the eighties. They are big Molly Ringwald fans. Oh, and Bill Murray. I think they watch *Ghostbusters* and *Groundhog Day* at least once a year. I keep my opinions to myself and just go along with whatever they want to talk about."

"Can you give me their address?"

"I suppose. I'm going to feel bad if they're rude to you."

I smiled. "Don't worry about it. I can handle rude people now and then." I didn't enjoy talking to rude people, but I could do it if I had to. After the way my aunt treated me when I first got here, I figured I could take most things.

Darcy copied something off her phone and handed me a paper. "Here it is. Take Boyd with you."

I shook my head. "Why does everyone always tell me to take Boyd? If I ever find myself in trouble, I'm not sure he'll be much help."

"Of course I'm a lot of help," Boyd said, entering the kitchen. "I took karate back in 1982." He grinned and snatched another cookie. I would be the reason everyone in Muddy Creek got diabetes.

"Is your game over?" I asked.

"Yep. It didn't last long. We're too experienced for it, I guess."

"Do you want to go with me to talk to Patrick's parents? It looks like they live in a place called Haysville."

Boyd tucked in his plaid shirt. "I know Haysville. It's about ten miles from Wichita."

"Are you free today?"

"Yep. Marla wants to talk to you, though."

I found Marla still sitting with Barbra and Opal. "Hey, Marla. Thanks for coming by again. When did you take that picture?"

"Yesterday afternoon. It was the same as before. I wasn't able to catch up to him."

"Thanks for snapping the picture."

"Sure thing. I could have texted it to you, but I like this diner. It's worth the drive."

My face lit up. "Thank you."

"Sure thing, honey. I'll let you know if he pops up again. I hope he does because these cookies are delicious."

Chapter 10

Patrick's parents lived in a small rambler nestled behind some trees. We parked on the street and walked down the long, curvy driveway.

"Do we suspect the parents?" Boyd asked.

"No," I said. "I'm just hoping they know something. I don't know why they wouldn't tell the police if they did, though. It's probably a waste of time, but I want to make sure I try."

"If Marla has seen Patrick two times, we should probably hang around Wichita."

"But it's an immense place. There's no way we would find him."

Boyd nodded. "True, but she's seen him twice, so he probably hangs out in the same area."

"You're right."

"So, another stakeout?" Boyd was hopeful. "The last one was too short."

"Maybe."

We walked up to the house, and I rang the doorbell. After a minute, the door opened and a woman who looked about sixty opened it. "Yes?"

"Are you Mrs. Henderson?"

She pushed a piece of grayish-brown hair behind her ear. "Who are you?"

"My name is Ivy Clark, and this is Boyd Webster. I wanted to ask you about your son."

"Go away," a thin man with silver hair said, coming up from behind her.

He started to shut the door, so I stepped forward and talked fast. "Someone in Wichita said they saw Patrick."

The man frowned and paused. "You have one minute."

"A woman Patrick used to work with saw him twice this week. She even took a picture."

The woman looked down, and the man scratched his head.

"I work with Darcy in Muddy Creek. I'm trying to help."

The man came out onto the porch, and we stepped down to get out of the way. His wife joined him.

"We know Darcy is hoping for the best, but she's delusional," Mr. Henderson said. "I will never believe Patrick is running around Wichita while his family worries about him."

"But what if he is?"

Mrs. Henderson frowned. "Then we don't want to see him, anyway. If he's inconsiderate enough to put us through misery, then we don't care to see him."

"There could be a reason he isn't contacting you. If we could find him—"

"Let me see the picture," Mr. Henderson said.

I pulled out my phone, found the picture, and handed it to him. He squinted down at it. Mrs. Henderson poked her head over to get a glimpse.

"This isn't a good enough picture to prove anything," Mr. Henderson said. "It looks like someone found a man with red hair, snapped a picture, and decided it was him."

Mrs. Henderson rubbed her temples. "Why do people keep coming by to talk about Patrick?"

I shared a confused look with Boyd. "When was the last time someone came by?"

"There was that sheriff a few days ago and then a man who wouldn't share his name."

Boyd's eyes narrowed. "That sounds suspicious. What did he look like?"

She shrugged. "The man was tall, that's all I know. He was wearing a jacket with the hood up. He asked if we'd heard anything about Patrick lately. When he wouldn't give his name, I slammed the door."

"You said you work with Darcy?" Mr. Henderson asked.

I nodded. "Yes, I own the diner she works at."

"So you aren't with the police or anything. You're just a diner owner."

"Well, yes, but we have solved a mystery before."

He frowned and shook his head, and she crossed her arms. I didn't impress them in any way.

"I can do things the police can't. I'm not tied to their rules."

Mr. Henderson sniffed. "So you're making your own rules and hoping to get somewhere?"

"Sometimes you have to cross the streams and see what happens." I knew I was going out on a limb here.

His eyes widened. "What do you mean, cross the streams?"

I shrugged. "It's like on *Ghostbusters*. Sometimes you have to do something you don't know will go well and hope for the best."

"That's so true," Mrs. Henderson said, looking at her husband. "Maybe she can do something."

"I don't know," he muttered, rubbing his chin.

"But her logic is sound, dear."

"I suppose so."

I forced myself to keep a serious expression. I couldn't believe one line from a movie was changing their opinion. It didn't even make sense; I was just grasping at straws.

"Why don't you come in?" she said, holding the door. We walked into a sitting room, and she pointed at the couch. "Sit."

We sat down, and the two of them took the loveseat.

Mrs. Henderson turned to me. "Did you know that a lot of Bill Murray's lines were improvised in *Ghostbusters*? The man is a genius."

"I didn't."

Mr. Henderson rolled his eyes. "Kids these days just like to be entertained and not know what goes on behind the scenes."

I hid a smile. I hadn't been called a kid in some time.

"So about Patrick..." Boyd said.

Mrs. Henderson sighed. "Right, Patrick. Something wasn't right the last month he was around. He never said what it was, but I could tell. We've concluded that he was killed, or he got into some kind of trouble and had to go into hiding."

I nodded. "Would he do that without telling anyone?"

"If he thought he was protecting us, he would."

"Can you think of anything he might have gotten mixed up in?"

Mr. Henderson's mouth turned down. "No. If we knew anything, we would have told someone sooner." He looked down at the phone. "Is there any way to make the picture bigger?"

I stood and went over. I took the phone and zoomed in closer. It only made it more blurry. I handed it to him, and he stared at it. His eyes widened, and he looked at his wife. Her lips were pressed together in a tight line.

"I think you should go," he said, stuffing the phone in my hand. "Don't come back, and drop this entire thing now. You're going to get in over your head."

Chapter 11

I scooped out a few teaspoons of cinnamon and dumped them into my mixing bowl. Today was the first day of the festival, and I was making pumpkin chocolate chip muffins to sell at one of the booths. I wasn't actually operating the booth because Livy volunteered. These were one of my favorite desserts, so I'd saved them until October. I hoped people would buy them at the festival and then come to the diner for more.

The diner smelled like pumpkin and cinnamon because I'd been making them all morning. I turned on the mixer and watched it all come together. I poured in a few cups of chocolate chips and smiled. These muffins would be perfect, and I hadn't sampled a single one. I shouldn't give myself credit for that because they tasted better once they were cool.

I'd taken Jett's advice and closed the diner for the day. My employees could all have a break, and I had time to bake. Creepers ran around the kitchen, trying to trip me as he hunted for mice or bugs. Everyone talked about mice problems, but I had yet to see one. I had seen Creepers take down a few bugs, which I appreciated.

Someone tapped on the back door, and I unlatched the two new locks Jett had installed. I now had more locks on the diner and my room than I knew what to do with. He also had someone put up extra lights on the outside and cameras pointing at both doors.

Jett stood on the porch holding a pumpkin. "Hey, I brought this for the counter."

"Thank you!" I said, taking it from him. "I looked for one yesterday and couldn't find any. Everyone said the same. Come back tomorrow."

"Well, there are plenty now. What's that smell?" Jett asked, squinting into the kitchen.

"Pumpkin chocolate chip muffins."

"For the festival?"

"Yes."

He winked at me. "Do you need a taste tester?"

I stepped back and let him enter. I shut the door and smiled. "Yes. You might need to test one from each batch to make sure I didn't forget the salt or anything."

"I am definitely the man for that job."

I handed him a muffin. "I thought you might be."

He took a bite and closed his eyes. "Mmm. These are going to be a hit."

"I hope so. I told Livy she could have all the profit for when she goes to college."

"These are going to sell out. Are you going to sell them each week?"

"Yes, and I'll start having them at the diner for the rest of the month. I'm thinking of adding seasonal desserts, so this will be my trial run."

"Nice. I just saw Matt Hooper. He's still at the top of my list of suspects."

"He seemed nice to me. I know people can act, but I'm also leaning toward believing Marla."

Jett took another bite and looked thoughtful. "She's on my list. It seems odd that she would see him twice after you started looking. I've sent Patrick's picture to the police. They have a station right near his old job, so they're watching for him."

"We really need to find out if he's still alive. I think that narrows things down a lot. If he's alive, then he left on his own. If he's dead, it has to be Marla because she's the one who keeps saying she saw him. I think that either way, that clears everyone around here."

Jett sat on a stool. "That makes sense, but what if Marla saw someone who looked like Patrick? She said he was heavier. And Boyd said Patrick's parents didn't think the picture was him."

"I don't know. They were acting really weird. Something in the picture bothered them."

"It could have been a look-alike or a relative. Darcy said he has a brother."

"But he's in jail."

"Do we know that for sure? I don't think Darcy talks to Patrick's parents very much. He might be out by now."

I nodded. "Is that something you can check?"

"Yeah, I'll make a call. I actually didn't think about it until just now. Sometimes I need to talk things out before they make sense."

A pounding on the door startled me. Whoever was knocking really wanted to get my attention. The doorbell began ringing, and I wondered if it was a kid. No one else would push it so many times.

Jett followed me to the front door, and we saw Boyd peering in with his hands up to the glass.

I unlocked the door and let him in. "What is it, Boyd?"

"I just saw Patrick Henderson."

Jett put his hands on Boyd's shoulders. "Are you positive?"

"Yep. It was him, alright." Boyd wore a black sweater with pumpkins going around the middle. "When he saw me, he went behind Hal's shop."

"I'm going to look," Jett said. "You two stay here."

I wanted to argue, but there wasn't time for that. If Patrick knew someone was looking for him, he might not hang around for long. Jett turned and jogged away from the diner.

"I guess we solved it," Boyd said. "It smells good in here."

"Come have a muffin." We went to the kitchen, and I handed him a cool one. "I'm not sure it's solved. We still don't know where he was and why."

"Once Jett catches him, he'll have to talk."

"I wonder if I should have warned Darcy."

"About what?"

"About Patrick being alive."

"But you just found out."

"Yes, but we suspected."

I took a muffin pan and began filling it with batter. "No. I didn't want to tell her until we were sure."

He bit his muffin and shook his head. "Darcy will be crushed. I can't believe this from Patrick. If he's no good, he fooled us all."

"It would seem that way."

We talked while we waited for Jett. It felt like an eternity before he came back in. When he did, his mouth was in a tight line and his brows were together.

"Any luck?" I asked.

He took a muffin. "Nope. I looked all over the square, between all the buildings. If he came here, there must be a reason. I'm going to jump in my truck and drive around for a while. I don't think we can keep this a secret. We need people to be on the lookout for him."

"Do you want me to go tell Darcy?"

"Tell me what?" Darcy asked, entering the kitchen. I hadn't heard the bell on the door.

The three of us all shared looks.

"What is it?" she asked, clasping her hands together. "I can take it."

Boyd cleared his throat. "I just saw Patrick."

Her eyes went wide. "You saw him? But... how... where?"

"He was over by Hal's."

Jett stepped forward. "I tried to find him, but I couldn't."

"I need to go home," Darcy muttered. "If he's here, he'll come for me. I don't want him to go and not find me." She turned and hurried off.

"I'm not sure it's safe for her," Jett said. "Boyd?"

"I'll go with her." He rushed after her.

"What should I do?" I asked. I glanced at the oven where my muffins were cooking.

"Stay here. I'll call you if I need anything."

I nodded and watched him leave. I grabbed a rag and wiped the counter. Creepers jumped up and began licking the cinnamon faster than I could clean it.

"Stop it, Creepers," I said, taking him off the counter. I'd learned really fast this morning that he loved the taste of cinnamon. I'd searched the internet and found that it wasn't horrible for cats in small amounts, but more than that should be avoided. He tried jumping up again, but I blocked him. "That isn't good for you."

He meowed near my feet, so I stopped and picked him up. I carried him outside in the front and decided we would take a little walk. It might be good to have multiple people looking for Patrick. Of course, all I'd seen was an outdated picture, but I was getting used to the people who regularly hung around town.

Creepers climbed onto my shoulder, and I put a hand on his back to keep him stable. The streets were emptier than usual. A lot of the businesses were closed today, and the owners were setting up stands to sell things. We walked around the block, then I checked on the muffins. I took Creepers upstairs so he could nap while I was at the festival.

Whatever was happening with Patrick wasn't sitting right with me. There was still the fact that someone had broken into my room and left that note. Patrick hadn't been spotted until recently, so he probably didn't leave it. Who else would care, though? I thought of Sally. Would she do it so that I couldn't find him?

I pulled the muffins from the oven and put the cool ones into containers. Livy would be by soon with her dad's truck to pick them up. I took the containers and stacked them all on the table closest to the door. When I'd placed the last container on the pile, I glanced at the door. A man with red hair stared back at me. I gasped and took a step back. It looked a lot like the picture of Patrick Henderson.

Chapter 12

Even though I'd been told the festival was huge, I hadn't been prepared for how massive it was. The two farms that hosted it were bursting with activities and vendors. Pumpkins and cornstalks had been placed in attractive arrangements that people could take pictures next to. There were rows and rows of booths selling everything from food to jewelry to 3D-printed items.

I left Livy to sell the muffins and walked around, searching for a familiar face. I was still annoyed that I hadn't thought fast enough when I saw Patrick. He'd smiled at me through the window, and I froze. By the time I had the door opened, he was gone. I was almost sure Patrick was up to no good. The smile he'd given me had been anything but friendly. I'd called Jett, but he hadn't been able to find him.

Boyd went riding by on his electric bike. He backtracked when he saw me and climbed off. He pulled off his green helmet and held it at his side. "Hey, we match!" he said, pointing at his orange pumpkin sweater.

I grinned. I was wearing a plain green long-sleeved shirt. "You have a strange idea of matching."

"Your necklace."

I wore a pumpkin necklace. "Oh, I see. That seems like a stretch."

"Why are you wandering around alone? Festivals are meant to be enjoyed with family and friends."

"You're the first person I recognized."

"Have you been in the maze yet?"

"No. I don't really want to go in alone."

"I would go with you, but I got so lost the last time I went in that it took me hours to get out. My legs aren't up for that."

"I'm sure there are other fun things."

"I saw Darcy and the queen at the petting zoo. They have some cute baby goats."

"I didn't think Darcy would be here."

"She's scanning the crowd. I think she's hoping Patrick shows up."

"Where are you off to?"

Boyd grinned. "The kissing booth, of course."

I laughed. "And who is running that?"

"Barbra and her pals."

"I need to see that."

"They do it every year. It's become a bit of a joke between me and those ladies. They always refuse to let me participate, but I'm not giving up."

"Who are you hoping to kiss?"

He winked at me. "I thought you were the detective here?"

I narrowed my eyes and tried to think. "I'm sure it isn't Opal. My money is on Barbra."

His eyes twinkled, and he laughed. "I've had my eye on Barbra since we were in our early sixties."

"How did I miss it?"

"Because you're too busy checking out the sheriff to see what everyone else is about."

I slapped him playfully on the arm. "You are horrible. I'm not checking out the sheriff."

"Maybe not this very moment, but I suspect that's because you don't know where he is."

"You have to stop teasing me about him. He's going to hear you one of these times."

He chuckled. "He wouldn't be surprised. Don't you think I probably tease him when you aren't around?"

My cheeks felt warm. "You better not." My eyes rested on a figure moving toward the corn maze, and I took a sharp breath. "Patrick."

Boyd turned. "Oh boy."

Patrick disappeared into the maze, and I looked around frantically. There was no sign of Jett. "I'm going after him. Find Jett." I turned and ran, not waiting for a response. I pushed my way past the people standing in line, ignoring the protests. Jett might have to arrest me because I didn't pay for a ticket. I rushed into the maze and paused when it split in two directions. I couldn't see anyone either way, so I picked one and ran as fast as I could.

The maze wasn't very crowded yet, but I still had to maneuver around people. After turning a corner, I decided I'd probably gone the wrong way, or I would have overtaken him unless he was running as well. I pivoted around and went in the other direction, passing the same people I'd already sped past. I slowed down and stopped when I heard arguing. They weren't being quiet, but I couldn't quite make out what was being said.

I walked slowly forward and peeked around a corner. Patrick and Matt stood glaring at one another. I took a step toward them, stepping on a dry cornstalk. They both turned and stared at me. Patrick darted off through the corn, not following the path. I don't know what Matt did because I was off again chasing Patrick.

He was easy to follow now because I had my eye set on him, and it was slow going through the dense corn. I wasn't sure what I would do if I caught up to him, but I would worry about that later.

"Ivy!" Matt called from behind me. I turned and saw him making his way through the corn. When I turned back to Patrick, he was gone.

"No!" I exclaimed, following the trampled stalks. After a minute, I ended up back on the path. I looked both ways and let out a frustrated growl. Where had he gone? I shouldn't have let Matt distract me. I thought I saw a flash of color turn a corner to the left, so I ran that way.

Every time I turned a corner, Patrick turned a different one. At least, I assumed it was Patrick. Who else would run? I mean, I guess I could have scared some innocent person when I came tearing around the corner, but what were the chances? I hadn't seen anyone else over here.

I hoped Patrick wasn't in great shape because I wouldn't be able to run much longer. I rounded a corner and faced a long, straight row. There was no one there. He must have run into the corn again.

Someone grabbed me from behind, pinning my arms and covering my mouth with their other hand. The pressure on my mouth was too hard to allow me to bite them. He pressed his face against mine as I struggled.

"Tell Darcy to move on," he said. "Leave the past buried." He pushed me to the ground and ran in the other direction.

By the time I was back on my feet, he had a good head start and was turning the corner. It was getting dark, so I needed to hurry. I ignored the stitch in my side and ran.

When I rounded the corner, I came to an abrupt halt. Patrick was on the ground, unmoving. Matt stood above him, holding a knife. When he saw me, he dropped it to the ground.

I covered my mouth with my hand and took a deep breath.

Matt held up his hands, his eyes wide. "Ivy, I know this looks bad, but I didn't do it."

I took a step back. "You were holding the knife!"

"I know, but it wasn't me! I came around the corner and saw him. A person dressed in black dashed into the corn. I just pulled the knife out of him, I swear."

I squatted next to Partick and clumsily felt his wrist for a pulse. I wasn't taking my eyes off Matt.

My eyes narrowed. "He's dead."

"I'm not going down for this," Matt said. He turned and ran.

"Great," I said, standing. Chasing him was out of the question. I was out of breath, and he was moving fast. I needed to get help, and I needed to do it before Matt could get far. Pulling my phone from my pocket, I frowned. No signal. I couldn't stay here and hope someone came. And what would I tell Darcy? I found her husband, and he wasn't dead, but now he was?

I grabbed a cob of corn and started walking through the maze, dropping corn kernels as I went. I wasn't sure how well anyone could follow it because there was corn all over the place. Every time I turned a corner, I put a small pile together so that it would at least be obvious I'd turned there.

A dark figure popped out in front of me, and I screamed. He was wearing a ski mask and black clothing. I remembered Jett saying the corn maze became a haunted maze once it was dark. It was probably only an actor.

"I need you to show me the way out," I said. "It's an emergency."

"Never," a man's deep voice said. I could tell he was going out of his way to disguise it. I still wasn't sure if it was an actor or not. Before I could run, he grabbed my wrist. Actors in haunted mazes aren't allowed to touch people.

"Let go, Matt. I already texted the sheriff, and he knows it's you," I lied.

He paused for a moment, and I punched him in the face. He released me and stumbled back. When he turned and started to retreat, I jumped on his back. In my mind, he had fallen, but in reality, he kept moving as he tried to pry my hands off him. I scratched his neck as I fell and watched him disappear into the night.

I sat for a minute, trying to decide my next move. I got up and brushed off my pants. I couldn't tell which way was which, and I didn't want to wander deeper into the corn. I stood and walked slowly in one direction, listening for any sign of another person.

"Ivy!" someone yelled.

"Here!" I called, turning toward the voice. A figure ran toward me. I wasn't positive in the dark, but I thought it was Jett. He shined a light on me, and I squinted.

"What are you doing?" It was definitely Jett. "What happened to you?"

I touched my hair and felt little sharp pieces of something. Perhaps hay or maybe cornstalk. "Patrick is dead."

He frowned. "I thought you said you saw him?"

"I did, but now he's dead. He's out here somewhere. I'm so turned around, and in the dark, I'll never find him again."

Jett put his arm over my shoulders, and we started walking. "Could you tell how he died?"

I shivered. "I didn't look closely, but Matt was standing over him with a knife."

"That's not good."

"That's an understatement."

"I guess it is." He sighed. "You're sure it was Matt?"

"Yes. He dropped the knife when I saw him and said it wasn't him. He said he pulled the knife out."

"Hmm."

"Then someone wearing a ski mask grabbed me."

He turned sharply and stopped. "What? Was it Matt?"

"I don't know. That was my first guess, but Matt wasn't dressed in all black, and he wouldn't have had time to change. I scratched whoever it was," I said, holding up my finger. "I'm not sure how hard it was, but maybe I got some of his skin under my nail."

We started walking again. "That was smart. Don't wash your hands. I don't have cell service, but once I do, I'll call in backup. I can't believe Patrick's been alive all this time and dies now."

"Before I found him, I overheard Patrick and Matt arguing. When they saw me, they took off. Then Patrick came up behind me and told me to tell Darcy to get over him or something like that. At least, I'm fairly certain it was him. I didn't see him. I'm not sure he was as nice and innocent as everyone portrayed him."

"It is getting more complicated."

I agreed. It wasn't the only thing getting complicated. Jett still had his arm around me, but I assumed it was because we were in a creepy dark cornfield, and I looked like I'd been in a fight.

"Don't forget and accidentally wash your hands before we check for DNA."

"I won't." I leaned in closer. It was cold, after all. He smelled like cinnamon. I wondered if that meant he'd been eating my muffins.

He rubbed my arm. "I wish I didn't have to tell Darcy."

Chapter 13

I sat on an uncomfortable chair in the police station in Wichita. Darcy sat next to me. She was leaning on her elbow, sleeping. She'd gone through a lot of emotions throughout the night. Knowing that Patrick had been alive was harder on her than learning he was now dead. Now she had to wonder why he'd been gone, why he'd come back, and why he had been acting violently.

Jett was still in Muddy Creek with a bunch of police officers looking for Patrick's body and for Matt. José had driven us here and was now out finding us something for breakfast. I was past tired, but I hadn't nodded off once. If there was a record of how many times a person could yawn in a minute, I might have it.

I'd given my statement more times than I could count, and a gruff man covered in tattoos and facial hair had cleaned my fingernails. He said I'd scratched the man hard enough, and they could test his DNA.

A woman we'd talked to earlier came in. She told us we could leave. I was relieved, but it would take some effort to get out of my chair.

I shook Darcy's shoulder, and her eyes opened. "It's time to go."

She nodded and got to her feet. I called José and told him to meet us out front. We waited until he pulled up, and Darcy climbed into the back quietly and slumped over. I got into the passenger's seat and buckled. José handed me a breakfast sandwich. He passed one back to Darcy, and she reluctantly took it. We drove in silence while we all ate.

I stared out the window and forced myself to stay awake. José hadn't slept, and I didn't want him driving drowsy while I slept.

Darcy pounded her fist against her seat. "This doesn't make sense. I knew Patrick, and he never would have left. Something happened. I don't know what it could be, but I know it. He was always a good guy, and he would never hurt anyone."

I didn't respond. Patrick would never hurt anyone? I rubbed my mouth. I could still feel where he'd held his hand tightly over it.

José glanced in the rearview mirror. "I'm sure it will all make sense someday."

Darcy let out a long breath. "I don't see how it could."

We spent the rest of the drive in silence. We dropped Darcy off at her house, then went to the diner. The Closed sign was on. I don't know why I was surprised. None of the cooks had been here at opening time, and no one else had a key.

A huge yawn made my jaw pop. "I say we stay closed for the day. We need to rest. I'll text everyone and tell them what happened—or some version of it."

I got out of the car and staggered to the diner. I pulled out my keys and tried to focus on them. It wasn't worth it. I sank down by the diner and leaned against the door, closing my eyes. I would just rest for a minute before I went inside.

The next thing I knew, someone was calling my name. I pulled open my eyes to see Jett running toward me.

"Ivy!" He exclaimed, kneeling next to me. "What happened?"

I blinked a few times and rubbed my cold arms. "Don't worry, I'm fine. I'm just resting for a moment before I go inside. My eyes can't focus on the keys."

He grabbed my hand and pulled me to my feet. "Give me the keys."

I handed them to him. "I'm sure I'll be fine in a minute."

He opened the door, and I stepped inside. "Have you been out here since José dropped you off?"

"Yeah, it's only been a few minutes."

"José called me four hours ago and told me he was home."

My eyes went wide. "I've been sleeping outside for four hours? In the middle of the day?" I frowned. "No one was concerned enough to come see if I was alright?"

He closed the door. "I haven't seen anyone around the square. I think everyone is recovering from the festival, plus it's Sunday, so almost nothing is open."

"Right, Sunday. We wouldn't have been open, anyway. I can't believe I was out here for four hours!"

"Come into the kitchen, and I'll see if I can heat something for you."

"Hot chocolate is all I want. I'm freezing. Why don't you look exhausted?" I asked as we entered the kitchen.

Jett looked at the floor and rubbed the back of his neck. "When the Wichita police came, they wanted me to stay in my office in case anything happened. I fell asleep and slept all night. I can sleep anywhere."

I sat on a stool. I couldn't fault him. What else was he going to do? He went over to the hot chocolate maker, filled it with water and cocoa, and flipped it on.

"Did the police find Patrick?"

"Nope. They can't find any sign of him being there. No body, no blood, nothing. They had a lot of officers out there, too. They went around this morning as well once it was light. For now, they are blocking off the area."

"Great. Everyone is going to think I'm crazy."

"No, something definitely happened. Matt is MIA, making him look even more suspicious. No one can find him, and he isn't answering his phone. Brian's pretty upset."

"Matt looks pretty guilty, but I have to wonder what Patrick was up to. I hope I'm not the reason all of this happened. Maybe if I'd left things alone, Patrick would have stayed missing."

"How would he have known? If someone told him you were looking into it, they would have had to know he was alive."

"I wonder how hard it would be to talk to his brother in prison. Maybe Patrick was secretly involved with some things his brother was, but he never got caught. I keep meaning to find out why his brother is in jail, but I don't know his name, so I can't google him or anything."

"I made a few calls this morning to see if he was still incarcerated."

"Oh?"

"He's still locked up. He hasn't had any visitors in a couple of years. His parents tried to talk to him, but he refused to meet with them. Oh, and his name is Quinn Henderson."

"What is he in for?"

"Embezzlement and attempted murder."

"Interesting. Who did he try to kill?"

"His boss. He found out Quinn was embezzling from the company and threatened to turn him in. The money was never found, so they believe an accomplice is out there somewhere. Whoever it was is keeping quiet, and Quinn won't talk."

I tapped my fingers against my leg. "I wonder if it was Patrick. That might be the reason he disappeared. He took the money and ran."

"It makes sense, but why wait to run until five years ago? His brother had already been in prison when he met Darcy."

I nodded. "I still don't get how they didn't find Patrick. Did someone move the body? I don't understand. I ran around a bit in there, but I couldn't have gotten so far in that people wouldn't find him. Plus, he was on the path, so someone should have a map or something."

"They do have a map. They combed the entire area, but there was nothing. They also had a drone fly over." He turned off the hot chocolate maker and poured some into a mug. "Here you go."

I took the mug and held it against my chilly hands. "Thanks."

"I'll run up to your room and make sure Creepers has food and water."

I sipped the hot drink. "Thank you." I felt better than I had, but I was still tired.

A few minutes later, he came back holding Creepers. "He must have missed you. He didn't want to stay up there."

I put the mug down, and he handed me my cat. I put my head down so he could rub his head into mine. "Did you miss me?" He purred.

Jett opened a drawer and pulled out a dishrag. He got it wet and began wiping the island where I made the muffins yesterday. I'd cleaned most of it up, but not all.

"You don't need to do that."

He grinned. "I know. Just pet your cat and drink your hot chocolate."

"I love you so much right now."

He turned his back and kept scrubbing. I knew I was imagining it, but it sounded like he muttered, "I wish."

Chapter 14

"Why do you want to talk to Sally?" Boyd asked two days later. "It sounds like the person who attacked you was a man, and probably Matt."

I handed him a plate of fried eggs and bacon. "I'm beginning to wonder if this is all far more complicated than I thought. What if a lot of people are involved? What if Matt is part of it, but someone else is, too? I'm finding it hard to believe Matt could be the one I scratched, but he was one hundred percent the one holding the knife."

Boyd sat in the kitchen's corner and ate. He'd come in to help in the kitchen while Darcy was out. She'd asked to have a week or two to gather herself. Boyd wasn't the best cook, but he could follow directions, so it was working so far today. The diner wasn't very busy, so he was taking a break.

José put whipped cream on a waffle and sent it out to the servers. "I know Darcy and Sally have a complicated relationship, but I don't think Sally would team up with Matt. She never liked him."

I nodded. "Which means she wouldn't mind if he took the fall."

"But wouldn't she worry about going down with him?" Boyd asked.

"I don't actually think she's involved, but I want to be thorough. It's still driving me mad they haven't found the body. It makes me look crazy."

"No one thinks you're crazy," José said. "Everyone is talking about Matt and blaming him. The police are looking for him, and even his family wonders about him. Brian didn't come out and say it, but from the way he talked yesterday, I think he believes Matt is guilty."

"Well, I'll feel better when it's all over. On a happier note, I have a few people who have applied for jobs here."

José grabbed a carton of eggs from the fridge. "Hallelujah. It would be nice to have shorter shifts."

"I was wondering if you might want to interview them. I'm still getting used to running a restaurant, and I bet you would be better at choosing suitable candidates."

José glanced over at me and grinned. "I would love that."

"Great. I'll give you the applications, and you can set up interviews whenever it works for you."

"Awesome. Thank you."

"Sure. You're really doing me a favor, though. So are you guys alright with me going to talk to Sally?"

"Take Boyd with you," José said.

"I can't leave you here, cooking by yourself."

"It's Monday. I'll be fine."

"Is that alright with you, Boyd?"

"Yep," Boyd said, putting his dish in the sink. "I don't like to be left out of these things."

I paused after I grabbed my purse. "Do you think Darcy will be alright with us going there? I don't want to upset her."

Boyd shrugged. "She's already upset. I don't see how it can get any worse."

When we arrived at Sally's house, she was sitting outside on her porch in a wooden rocking chair. She glared at us as we approached her.

"I already talked to the sheriff. I suppose you're coming to snoop now, as well."

I leaned on the porch railing. "The sheriff was here?"

She took a swig from a glass bottle at her side. "Sure was. He wanted to know how Darcy was doing. He asked me more questions than was normal. If I didn't know better, I'd think he thought I killed Patrick. What would I gain from that?"

"So you liked him?"

"Of course not. I don't like anyone. Still, he was more useful to me alive. He took care of Darcy, and you know how needy that girl is."

I raised my brow. I'd seen how hard Darcy worked, and I was sure she was the one who kept everything afloat at home. Sally couldn't do much with her arthritis, and the house and yard were well kept. I knew that was all Darcy.

"You don't like Darcy living here?"

"Sure I do. It would be nice if someone took care of Netty, though. That girl complains about everyone and everything. I don't know where she gets it. Darcy was never a complainer."

Boyd grinned, and I hoped he wouldn't say anything to insult her.

"Do you ever leave the house?" I asked. "I've never seen you in town."

She rolled her eyes. "Why would I go to town? I can have pretty much everything delivered, and I don't have to talk to anyone. That is the way I like it. The last time I went to town, I got into a fight with your no-good uncle. Thank goodness I don't have to deal with him anymore. I got Hal to come fix a shelf in my garage last week. Karl came and fixed some wires under my crawl space. Jaycee painted my fence. Darcy does everything else. I don't need town."

I had nothing to say to that.

"Do you have any guesses as to what happened to Patrick?" Boyd asked. I guess he was tired of me trying to get there slowly.

"It all seems pretty cut-and-dried to me. Matt Hooper killed him in the corn maze. That's what everyone is saying."

I wondered who the everyone she was referring to was. She just admitted she didn't talk to people.

"Do you really think Matt would do it?" Boyd asked.

"Come now, Boyd. You've known Matt Hooper all his life, just like I have. When has he ever been a good citizen? From what I hear, Ivy is the one who saw him standing there with a knife. What other conclusion could come from that?"

"When was the last time you talked to Matt?" I asked.

"Hmm. It's been years. I can't really say exactly. I never liked him when Darcy dated him, so there certainly wasn't any reason to talk to him once they broke up. Why is everyone asking me questions? You think I conspired with the killer and let him bury Patrick under my shed or something?"

"No. I guess we'll be going," I said. This was a waste of time.

"Next time, call before you come."

I nodded.

We said goodbye and got in the car.

Boyd chuckled. "Sally has always been a ray of sunshine."

"I don't think she had anything to do with Patrick."

"Me neither. Now what?"

I blew out a long breath. "I want to go to the prison and talk to Patrick's brother."

"Now?"

"Soon. I'm not sure how that all works. I don't know if I need an appointment or permission, or what."

"You could ask Jett to arrange it."

"I doubt he knows how. It's not part of his job." We drove down the dirt road in thought. I wondered if Quinn would even agree to see me. If he did, what would I even say? Darcy didn't seem to know anything about him, and he was obviously dangerous unless prison had changed him.

When we got back to the diner, José had everything under control. Only two tables had people, and they were talking quietly to one another. I should make José a manager. He makes better decisions than I do when it comes to the diner, and he knows how everything works. If I could hire more cooks, he would have time to do something like that. He did a lot more than he was hired to do, anyway.

Boyd told José what Sally had said and about my plan to go to the prison.

"You can get an appointment at the prison if the prisoner wants to talk to you," José said. "I had a cousin who was locked up for a year, and my mom went in a few times and visited him. I can call her after work and ask her what you should do."

"That would be great, thanks. I need to clear my head. Are we short on any desserts? I think I'm in the baking mood."

"I think we're set for the rest of the day unless you want to make some pumpkin muffins. People have been talking about them."

"That's right. I was going to make sure we had them all month. I'll get some going."

The bell above the door chimed. I glanced through the kitchen window to see Jett enter. He came straight to the kitchen.

"Hey, everyone. I just got a call from Wichita. The DNA from Ivy's fingernail does not match Matt Hooper."

I put a hand to my heart. "Are they sure? Matt was standing there with the knife." That made me think again about multiple people being involved.

Jett shrugged. "Either Matt was telling the truth, and he didn't kill Patrick, or he has an accomplice."

Boyd raised his hand. "Or there are just a bunch of people who didn't like Patrick, and he fooled the rest of us."

"There is also the fact that Matt didn't attack Ivy in the maze when she saw him with the knife. He could have."

I started tossing things into the mixer. "What if this is a lot bigger than we think? It's like I was saying earlier. I really wonder if Patrick was involved in something big and something related to his brother being in jail. I really need to talk to his brother."

"Quinn Henderson has been in prison for a long time. It's obvious he hasn't been communicating with people. They keep records at the prison."

"Did the DNA have a match?" I asked.

"No. The man I talked to said that they thought someone might have tampered with the system, but he wouldn't tell me anything besides that."

I took a deep breath. "What if Matt really was just an innocent bystander?"

Boyd shook his head. "I doubt it. They were fighting, and then he was found holding the knife? That screams guilty."

"But what if he isn't? If the DNA doesn't match, that means someone else threatened me."

Chapter 15

"You're lucky Quinn agreed to see you," a woman at the prison told me as she led me to a meeting room. Her name tag said Rachel. "He hasn't agreed to see anyone in years. What's your connection to him?"

I shrugged. "I don't know him, but I have some information about his family he might want to know."

"Interesting. He won't even see his parents. He's a curious case."

"How so?" I asked as we walked down a long white hall.

"Well, he rarely interacts with anyone. He does what he's told, and in his free time, he exercises or reads. He's never been a problem in the three years I've worked here."

Rachel opened a door and motioned for me to enter. A man sat on a chair that was bolted to the floor. He was handcuffed to one side, and he was reading a book.

He had red hair that went to his shoulder and a bushy red beard that disappeared into his orange jumpsuit. His shoulders were broad, and his jumpsuit was tight against well-defined biceps. He looked up when we entered and closed his book. He had a small scar near the corner of his eye.

The woman motioned to a chair ten feet away from Quinn. I sat down and shifted nervously. The man's eyes never left my face, making me feel self-conscious.

"I'll be watching through the mirror," the woman said, pointing at a mirror on the wall. "Raise your hand if you want me to come in. Say what you want. I have no interest in listening." She stuck some earbuds in her ears and left the room.

I fidgeted and wondered how to start. It was nerve-wracking the way he stared at me without blinking.

"Who are you?" Quinn asked. "I don't normally allow people to visit, but I was curious."

"My name is Ivy Clark. I run a small diner in Muddy Creek."

He sighed and slumped back. "Go on."

"I'm not sure if you've heard about your brother?"

His brows came together. "I know he's been missing."

I swallowed hard. "I'm sorry to be the one to tell you this, but he's dead."

Quinn leaned forward, resting his elbows on his knees. "How?"

"There was a festival, and he was in the corn maze. Someone stabbed him."

His eyes narrowed. "Why was he even in Muddy Creek? He shouldn't have been there."

"Why not? His wife and daughter are there."

"How long was he in town?"

"I'm not sure. A few people spotted him, and then he was killed."

"So he wasn't living there?"

"No."

He rubbed a hand over his eyes and rested his forehead on his hand. "Who killed him?'

"No one knows. It's complicated."

"How so?"

"A man was seen standing over him holding a knife, but the DNA doesn't match."

"I'm feeling lost here. What DNA?"

I wrung my hands in my lap. "I found Patrick and saw the man with the knife. When I was trying to get out of the maze, a man grabbed me. We assume it's the same man who killed Patrick, but I scratched him, and his DNA didn't match the man with the knife."

I wished he would blink. He just kept his gaze on me. "Did they do an autopsy?"

"No. They can't find his body."

"So all anyone knows is that you said you saw him dead?"

"The man with the knife also disappeared, and no one can get ahold of him."

"Hmm. What was that man's name?"

I wasn't sure I should give him all this information. "I'm not sure."

He gave me a half smile. "Liar."

"I…"

"Don't worry about it. You have no reason to trust me. So why are you here? The woman who runs the diner isn't usually the person who comes to tell an inmate they don't know that their brother died."

I looked at my hands. "I feel responsible. Patrick's wife asked me to help her find him. I stuck my nose in it, and then Patrick suddenly appeared and was killed. I wonder if he came back because he knew I was trying to find him. He was obviously involved in something sketchy." I looked up at him. "I was hoping you might know what that was."

He leaned back against his chair and stared up at the ceiling. "This is a mess. I don't think I can help you. My best advice would be to stay out of it. At least one dangerous person is out there trying to cover something up. If you keep getting involved, they might come for you."

"The sheriff has reopened the case along with the Wichita police."

He held the seat of his chair and nervously drummed his fingers against it. "You should try to convince everyone to let it go. Sure, he was killed, but that makes the world a better place."

"It's really confusing. Everyone I've talked to loved Patrick... Well, there were a few exceptions, but their dislike wasn't for valid reasons. When I met him, he was creepy and threatening. He was obviously hiding things."

"More than you can wrap your mind around. He should've been locked in here."

I leaned forward. "Can't you tell me anything that might help? If we know what he was up to, then we might be able to figure out who killed him and make sure they don't hurt anyone else." I realized I was appealing to an attempted murderer, but what else could I do? I had a feeling Quinn was involved somehow, and I was going to figure it out.

"Sorry. I can't think of anything. My brother and I were never close."

I narrowed my eyes and watched as he continued to drum his fingers against the chair. He knew something, and he wasn't telling me. Thinking a hardened criminal was going to pour out his secrets to me had been delusional.

I stood and looked for my purse. I'd forgotten they had kept it up front.

"Has anyone bothered Darcy and Netty?" he asked.

"No."

"Netty's got to be eight by now. What's she like?"

I sat back down and tried to think of something nice to say. "She's very committed to the things she believes in."

He scratched the back of his neck. "What does that mean?"

I smiled. "She tries to have everyone who goes against anything she believes in arrested. If you ever meet her, make sure you never sneeze. That really irritates her. The entire town would be in prison if the sheriff arrested everyone she asked him to."

Quinn laughed. "I wish I could see that."

"Have you ever met her?"

He shook his head. "No. I've been here for ten years."

"I'm not allowed to call her Netty. You have to be on fantastic terms with her for that."

"She sounds... interesting."

I realized I was being negative. "She's a cute little thing and smart. I think she spends too much time with her grandma."

His eyes narrowed. "Not my mom."

"No, Darcy's. Darcy has to work a lot, so Sally watches her."

He ran a hand over his face and muttered something. "She shouldn't have to work that hard."

I put a hand to my chest as my brain made sense of our conversation. I didn't know how I would ever unravel all of this without help. Quinn cared way too much about Netty and Darcy.

"What's going on?" I ask him.

His mouth turned down. "What do you mean?"

"Why are you here, Patrick?"

Chapter 16

I wasn't one hundred percent certain that Quinn was really Patrick, but his eyes went wide and teared up.

"We're done," he said.

"No. If you signal for Rachel to come in here, I'm going to tell her."

"You're grasping at straws. There is no way I could be Patrick. I've been here forever."

"But somehow you are."

He leaned forward, his eyes firmly fixed on me. "You need to go home and take care of your diner, and mind your own business."

"That's what the note someone left on my bed said."

He rolled his eyes. "That's what anyone would say to you. You already said you felt guilty about some things. Don't make it worse. Don't put Darcy in danger."

"How did you get here?"

"Search it online."

"Not Quinn. You. How did you get here, and how did Quinn get out? Why did he go to Muddy Creek, and who killed him?"

"This is insane. Do you always meddle in people's lives?"

"I'm trying to help my friend."

"You will help her more by leaving things alone."

"Were you and Quinn twins?"

"I'm not a twin and neither was Patrick. There's a year between us."

"You must look enough alike that people can't tell the difference. Marla and Boyd both thought he was you."

"Please, leave."

I could tell he wasn't going to admit to anything, so I stood. "Goodbye, Patrick. Get a message to me if you ever decide to come clean." I turned and waved at the mirror, and Rachel came and let me out.

On the drive home, I went over our conversation in my head. I wasn't one hundred percent sure he was Patrick, but I really thought he was. He didn't take me as a hardened criminal type. The man who had been killed in the corn maze had seemed to lean more that way. I wasn't sure what I should do when I got back.

If I told Jett about my suspicions, he would have to act. It was his job, and I knew he would follow the rules. He would probably have the prison fingerprint Quinn or

Patrick to see if they had the wrong brother. It was what I would probably do, but I was also worried about Darcy. If he was Patrick, he was choosing to stay where he was. He must have a reason, and it must be a good one.

There was also the chance I was wrong. If I was, Quinn probably thought I was a crazy person. I couldn't be wrong, though. Quinn and Patrick didn't get along and hadn't kept in touch. He wouldn't care about Netty and what she acted like. Darcy hadn't even known Quinn's name, so why would he know Netty's? I'd also seen his eyes tear up. I had to be right.

By the time I got to the diner, I had convinced myself beyond all doubt. Now I needed to figure out what to do with that information. I greeted some patrons as I walked past them and went into the kitchen.

José was training a new cook that he'd hired the day before. His name was Anton, and he was only twenty-five. I hoped he was qualified because José needed the help. He had also hired a woman I didn't know, but she didn't start until tomorrow. Boyd was still helping until they were trained. He was making a salad.

I wanted to talk to José and Boyd, but I couldn't do it in front of Anton.

"Hey, Ivy. The sheriff was in here looking for you," Boyd said. "When we told him where you were, he said to have you come talk at his office."

"Why did you tell him where I was?" I didn't want to explain myself to Jett.

He grinned. "Because he asked. You don't want me lying, do you?"

"Of course not." I noticed Anton watching me. That was one thing that would be annoying about having more employees. I would have to watch what I said more often. I glanced at my phone to check the time. The diner would close in an hour. "After I talk to the sheriff, I'm going to head over to Darcy's. Do you want to come?"

"Yep," Boyd said. José was showing Anton how to do something, but he gave me a small nod.

When I was leaving, I saw Creepers walking around the diner, trying to find someone to pet him. Everyone had been right. No one seemed to mind a cat wandering around the place. I picked him up and took him with me.

When I opened the door to the sheriff's office, I almost bumped into Karl Lattmire. I wondered if Jett had been asking him questions about driving to work with Patrick. Creepers reached out and batted at him. I needed to get him to stop doing that.

"Sorry about that."

He pulled his coat tight. "No problem."

Creepers hissed, and I turned him away. Karl nodded at me as he stepped out.

Jett sat at this desk, typing something on his laptop. I sat in a wooden chair that faced the desk and waited. He looked up. "Hang on just a second."

I set Creepers on my lap and ran my hand over his fur. He purred and closed his eyes.

Jett closed his computer and looked up at me. "Ivy, Ivy, Ivy," he said like I was a naughty toddler. "What do you think you were doing by going to talk to Quinn Henderson?"

I shrugged. "That he might know something."

He let out a long breath. "And did he?"

"I don't know. He said he didn't, but I think he's lying."

"Why?"

I absentmindedly stroked Creepers's back. "Just a gut feeling. Maybe you should go talk to him."

He sat back in his chair and studied me. "Is there something you're not telling me?"

I swallowed. I didn't want to tell him my suspicion. Lying was out of the question because I cared about what Jett thought about me. "Yes, but I'm not going to tell you."

He raised a brow. "What? You know something, and you aren't going to let me in on it?"

I moved my lips from side to side and tried to think my way out of this. "I don't know anything. I suspect something, but I don't want to tell you because you will feel obligated to find out if I'm right, which could cause problems."

He placed his elbows on the desk and blew out a breath. "I wish you would tell me."

"I can't. It doesn't matter, anyway. Right now, it's just a thought. I could be wrong, so there's no reason to bring it up."

"I wish you trusted me."

I tilted my head. "I do, but it's your responsibility to do your job to the best of your ability. I don't have that same responsibility, so I don't have to feel guilty about keeping this quiet until I'm sure things are safe."

"Safe? You can't keep a secret about things that might be dangerous."

Creepers jumped off my lap, and I watched him go under the desk. "I think it's more dangerous if it gets out."

Jett nodded. "Fine."

I could tell he was holding his anger in. I wondered if he would command me to tell him. He looked like he might. I wasn't sure if he was allowed to do that or not. Telling him would allow me to talk through my thoughts, but I was going to have to do that with Boyd, José, and Darcy.

"Why was Karl in here?" I asked. I wouldn't be surprised if he refused to answer me.

"I'm trying to talk to everyone who spent time with Patrick. I think I'm missing something."

"Any luck on finding Matt?"

"No. His car was found a few cities over, so the police there are keeping an eye out. Your cat is chewing on my boot."

I kneeled on the floor and looked under the desk. "Come here, Creepers." The cat reluctantly came to me, and I stood. "Is there anything else you need?"

He watched me with a blank expression. "No."

"Then I'll see you around. Tomorrow, I'm making pumpkin pie."

His face softened. "I'll be there."

I returned to the diner to leave Creepers and pick up José and Boyd. I was feeling a little guilty. Jett had looked almost hurt that I wouldn't share with him. Hopefully, he understood where I was coming from.

José, Boyd, and I got into my car, and we drove to Darcy's house. I guess it's really Sally's house, but I hoped we wouldn't have to deal with her today. When we pulled up, Netty came running over.

"Hi," she said as I exited the car. "What are you doing here?"

"We came to talk to your mom."

"She's out back picking the pumpkins. We have some big ones this year. I'm staying over here because we saw a snake, and I got scared. Come on. Maybe he's still out there." She took off running, and José, Boyd, and I followed.

Darcy was in a small pumpkin patch holding a little yellow pumpkin. She pushed her hair over her ear and smiled when she saw us. "Hello. Is there a problem at the diner?"

"No, but I need to talk to you."

"Should we go inside? My mom's already in bed."

"We can stay out here." I glanced over at Netty. I didn't want her overhearing anything. She might go tell Jett.

"Netty, why don't you go inside and figure out what we're eating for dinner?"

"Yay!" Netty yelled, running to the house.

Darcy placed the pumpkin near a bunch of others. "Has something happened?"

"I went to the prison and talked to Patrick's brother, Quinn, today," I blurted out.

Her eyebrows rose. "He agreed to see you? That's peculiar. He won't even see his parents."

I bit my lip. "Did Patrick have a scar by his eye?"

"Yes, he got it when Quinn threw something at him when he was younger."

"I don't know how to say this... I think Patrick is alive."

Darcy gasped, and José and Boyd gave me confused looks.

"I think Patrick is in prison, pretending to be Quinn."

Boyd shook his head. "That's even far-fetched for me."

I told them about my visit, and they all hung on my words. "I don't see any reason for Quinn to ask the questions he did. He had the scar, and he really seemed to care about what was happening with Netty."

Darcy blinked back tears. "I have no idea how that could even be possible, but I believe it. The Patrick you described in the corn maze was not my Patrick. I've been wondering how he could have fooled me, and he didn't. I need to go see him."

"I don't think that's a good idea. Not yet."

"But why? I need to get him out of there."

José patted her on the back. "Something strange must have happened to get him there. If he doesn't want anyone to know, there must be some reason. We need to be careful and figure this all out."

I nodded. "Jett knows I'm hiding something from him. I feel bad about it, but if we tell him, he'll have to check it out to see if it's true. We need to find out who killed Quinn and why. We also need to figure out how Patrick ended up in prison. I'm sure he was being threatened in some way. Maybe he still is, and that's why he doesn't want anyone to know who he is."

"Alright," Darcy said. "But it's going to be hard to stay here when I know where he is. I admit I feel some relief. I've been really upset, thinking he fooled me all those years. This makes me think he didn't leave of his own free will, and that's comforting in a way. Still, the poor guy. He's probably really been through something. I wish I could go to him."

"We're going to figure this out," I assured her. "Don't you worry."

Chapter 17

The following Saturday, the harvest festival was back on. A dance near the corn maze drew in a crowd. More police patrolled this time, and it looked like everyone was having a good time. I'd left Livy with the vendor's booth, and I was watching Boyd dance with Barbra. They danced across the straw, and I grinned. I wasn't sure what the purpose of the straw was, but it was all over the ground. Perhaps someone thought it was a cheap way to decorate.

The vendor booths formed a circle around the dancers and then went in two straight lines, making a path outside the corn maze. I didn't count, but I bet at least one hundred canopies were set up with people selling things. I hadn't looked too closely last time, so I wandered around, amazed at everything people had made. It's incredible what some people can knit and crochet. I wondered if I could pay one lady to make me a cat resembling Creepers.

I wasn't going to last long. It was only six o'clock, and I was freezing. I'd worn a cute blue sweater, but I was still cold. Growing up in Arizona, I'd rarely worn long sleeves, so I wasn't used to this. I should probably buy a coat.

"Hello!" a teenage girl greeted me. She was at a booth with some long metal—things. Pens maybe?

"Hi," I said, picking one up. It wasn't a pen, but I couldn't for the life of me figure out what it was. "What is it?"

"You put it in your hair."

"Ohhhhh." I remembered putting my hair in a bun and holding it up with a pencil in high school. I looked at the thirty-dollar price tag and raised my brows. I know people are trying to make money at these things, but that seemed steep for something a pencil could do.

"It's also for self-defense," the girl said, holding one up. "See, the end is pointed."

I touched the end and pictured myself pulling one from my hair and trying to stab someone. You would have to stab pretty hard to hurt someone with it. It was slightly sharp but not impressively so.

"Let me show you how to do it," the girl said, coming around her table.

"Oh, no thanks," I said. I'd curled my hair for this event and didn't want it messed up.

"Trust me," the girl said, going behind me and grabbing my hair. I sighed and waited while she took the top part of my hair and twisted it around. She stabbed one of her hairpins through it, then held out a mirror. It wasn't bad. She'd left most of my hair down, so it looked fancy. "I'll give you one for fifteen dollars if you act now."

Ah, so that was her game. "Alright," I agreed, pulling out my wallet. I probably shouldn't make eye contact with anyone here. I was obviously bad at saying no, so I'd be broke if every vendor sold me something. From the looks of it, there were a bunch of neat things. I handed her fifteen dollars and moved on.

"Why aren't you dancing?" Boyd asked, pulling me toward the dance floor. Well, it wasn't really a floor. It was dirt, but it served its purpose.

"I don't want to dance. It's too cold."

"Dancing will warm you up. It's a square dance, so it's perfect."

I gave in. If I had to dance, Boyd was a fun partner. I hadn't done this in years, but it came back quickly. I laughed as we danced around and found I was getting warmer. I was also having fun. Maybe one of the vendors was selling coats, and I could stay longer.

The music ended, and Boyd patted me on the back. "See? Wasn't that fun?"

"It was fun."

"Can I have the next dance?" a voice said behind me. I turned around to see Karl Lattmire. He didn't take me as the type to be out at the festival, let alone dancing.

I forced a smile. "Sure." Of course, it had to be a slow song. I took his hand and put one hand on his shoulder. I was surprised he knew how to dance, but he was good. My eyes fell to his neck, and I gasped. He had a scratch. It wasn't big, but it looked like something a person might get from... me.

"I need to talk to you," he said in a low voice.

I tried not to flinch. What if he had been the man in the corn maze?

"I have to admit something to you, but I hope you will keep it to yourself." His voice didn't sound threatening. He sounded worried.

My brows rose. "Oh?"

He sighed. "I'm the one who broke into your room."

I stopped dancing and released him. I opened my mouth to speak, but nothing came out.

"The truth is, Patrick actually talked to me when we drove to work. I think he figured that I'm not social, so I wasn't going to talk. He was involved in something. He didn't give me the exact details, but he owed money to someone dangerous. They'd threatened to hurt Darcy, and he was scared."

I crossed my arms for warmth and ignored the people dancing around us.

He looked down at the ground. "I thought about going to the police, but I didn't. I wish I would have. Patrick was worried Darcy might get hurt. He asked me to keep an eye on Darcy and Netty if anything happened to him. After he disappeared, I worried all the time. As time went by, I realized Darcy and Netty were probably safe. Whoever threatened Patrick must have been satisfied with whatever they did to him."

"But Patrick wasn't dead. Not until last week."

He shrugged. "I don't know how to explain that. All I know is that I panicked when you started asking me questions. I worried about trouble coming to Darcy and to you. That's why I broke in and left you that note."

"Why did you leave my window open?"

He kicked at the ground. "I felt like I needed to do something that would scare you. Just a little rain and the breeze blowing in sounded harmless enough."

"My cat could have gotten on the roof! I was terrified something happened to him."

"I'm sorry about that. He bit me, and I'm guessing he remembers me since he swiped at me the other day."

I would let him think that. Creepers swiped at anyone when he felt like it, including me.

"There is something else," he said. "Patrick borrowed money from Matt Hooper."

My eyes narrowed. "Why would Matt lend him money? Matt didn't like him."

"No, he really didn't, but I think Matt still cared enough about Darcy and was willing to help. I hope you won't tell the sheriff. I'm embarrassed enough as it is."

I clenched my fists. "Thanks for letting me know." I wasn't promising anything.

"You really need to let it rest. I don't want to see anyone else get hurt. I'm leaving tonight to go stay with my sister for a few days. She's remodeling and needs help. Here's my number if you need anything." He handed me a card, and I stuck it in my pocket. "I'll be a couple of hours away, but if you need me, I can come."

"Thank you."

I watched him walk away. Every time I thought it was complicated, something else happened.

"Hey, Ivy. What was Karl saying?" Jett asked, startling me.

I turned and tried to smile. "Uh, we were just talking."

He took my hand and put his hand on my waist. I tried not to smile as I placed my hand on his shoulder. I felt funny holding his hand. It reminded me of a sixth-grade dance position. It hadn't seemed strange with Karl, but with Jett, it did.

"Talking about what?" he pried.

"Just things."

His mouth turned down. "I don't think you should hang around him. There is something... off about him. I haven't figured it out yet."

I was feeling bold at the moment, so I released his hand and put my arms around his neck. His eyes widened, but he put his other hand on my waist. I grinned. "Are you sure you just don't want me dancing with him?"

He chuckled. "That might be part of it."

My smile faded. "Karl said he was the one who broke into my room."

His mouth turned down. "He told you?"

"Yeah." I told him everything that Karl had told me. I didn't want to be the only person who knew something. That might put Darcy and Netty in danger.

"So he did it to protect you?"

"That's what he said."

"Do you believe him?"

"No."

"Why?"

I stared up into his eyes. "He has a scratch on his neck. It could be a coincidence, or he could be the person from the corn maze. He didn't admit to being the one to scare me in there."

"Perhaps he thought you would just realize that was him as well. He could have been trying to scare you off to keep you safe."

"I guess."

"Well, whatever his motive is, stay away from him for now."

I nodded. "That won't be hard. There have only been two times I've seen him. I can't imagine what his motive could be if he is the one that killed Qu—Patrick." I hope he didn't notice my slip.

"Motives can be funny things. Sometimes it doesn't take much."

I shivered. My crazy moment of boldness was gone, or I would lean in. "How much colder is it going to get around here?"

"If you can't handle this, you better hibernate for the winter. It gets a lot colder. Do you have a coat?"

"I don't even have a jacket. It rarely gets cold enough to snow in Southern Arizona. I think I have a hoodie, but I didn't bring it."

The song ended, and I reluctantly dropped my arms. I really needed to get over this crush. I was pretty sure Jett considered me a friend. He might be a bit interested in me, but I wouldn't count on it.

He grabbed my hand, and we walked over to a hay bale. He grabbed his jacket from the top and handed it to me. "Take this."

"Then you'll be cold."

"Nah. This is nothing. I don't need it."

I pulled the khaki jacket over my arms and zipped it. It was too big, but better than freezing. "Thanks."

"I need to go do my rounds. I'll see you around."

My eyes scanned the crowd until they rested on José. He was eating a hot dog and talking to someone I didn't know. I walked toward him, and he ended his conversation and turned to me. "Hey, José. What are you up to?" It was a dumb question to ask someone at a festival, but I didn't want to pull him away if he was having a good time.

"I'm thinking about leaving. I'm only good for about an hour, and then I'm done."

"Do you want to go snoop around Karl Lattmire's house?"

José grinned. "You know it. Why Karl?"

"I'll tell you once we find Boyd."

"I'm here," Boyd said from behind me. "What's going down?"

"It sounds like we're going to spy on Karl," José said.

"Not spy on him. He's going to his sister's house, so his place should be empty."

Boyd scratched his head. "Did I miss something? Is he a suspect?"

"Yes. Maybe the top suspect."

Chapter 18

"Last time we tried something like this, it didn't go so well," Boyd stated as we sat in the car in front of Karl's house.

José laughed. "Just stay out of the trees, and we should be fine."

"Hey, sometimes you have to do curious things when you're looking for answers."

I smiled. "Climbing trees isn't going to be productive. Jett told me once that a lot of people around here don't lock their doors. Maybe we can try the doors."

José shook his head. "The more untrustworthy a person is, the more untrusting they are. I bet they're locked."

I'd told them about my conversation with Karl, but neither seemed to think he was the killer. Someone to avoid, but not the real bad guy in this situation. They still believed that to be Matt. I wasn't sure. If Matt had given Patrick money, that might have had something to do with the fight I witnessed in the corn maze. Money was a big motivator in a lot of fights. Maybe Matt got really mad and stabbed him... Well, stabbed Quinn.

We tried the front and back doors, and they were both locked. José went around, pushing on all the windows. I looked around for cameras. It always embarrassed me when I thought of Matt watching us snoop around his house. I couldn't see anything, and there were no blinking lights.

"Over here," José said. We all gathered under a window he had pushed open. "The lock is broken. It's too high for me to get in, but I can boost you."

"Alright." I took off Jett's jacket and handed it to Boyd. It was too bulky to let me move well.

"Isn't this the sheriff's jacket?" Boyd asked with a gleam in his eyes.

"I was cold."

Boyd laughed. "That's what every guy wants to hear."

I rolled my eyes and stepped into José's linked hands. He pushed me up, and I grabbed the windowsill and pulled myself through. The metal around the window dug into my stomach, causing me to hurry and fall into a dark room. I jumped to my feet and looked around. It was hard to see anything. I peered out the window, where José and Boyd stared up at me.

"I'll find the front door and let you in." I walked carefully across the unfamiliar room and into a hallway. A dim light glowed in a side room. I followed the hall toward the door. Thankfully, the house was small, so we wouldn't have too much space to deal with.

A sound in a room to the side made me freeze. I pressed myself against the wall and took a slow breath. I could wait for someone to pop out, or I could run for the door. It sounded like someone was rifling through things. I should have waited until I was sure Karl was gone.

I crept against the wall and peeked into the dark room. A person stood with his back to me, shining a flashlight into a filing cabinet next to a large desk. I couldn't see them clearly, but I was almost sure it was Matt.

"Don't move, or I'll shoot," I lied. He jerked up, his flashlight falling to the ground. He put his hands in the air. How had he not heard me fall in from the window?

"Ivy?" Matt asked from the darkness.

"Stay where you are," I said, trying to sound confident.

"What are you doing?" he asked, turning around. He frowned and dropped his hands. "You don't even have a gun."

"What are you doing here?"

"Trying to clear myself. You have to believe me when I tell you I didn't kill Patrick."

I tilted my head. "I might."

"You must think it's Karl too. Otherwise, you wouldn't be here."

A knock on the door made us both jump. "It's just José and Boyd. I need to let them in." Matt followed me to the door, and I opened it.

Boyd pointed at Matt. "What's he doing here?"

Matt crossed his arms. He was wearing gloves. "Probably the same thing as you."

"Did you find anything?" I asked.

"Maybe. I'm not sure. I was going through Karl's filing cabinet, and there was a bunch of mail addressed to someone named Gene Fletcher."

José crossed his arms. "Do you think he had a fake name?"

Boyd stepped inside. "Or he's stealing someone's mail."

Matt motioned for them to follow. "I think he has an alias. The mail is things like bills and stuff. Nothing anyone would want to steal."

"Well, I still think you killed Patrick," Boyd said. I shot him a look, and he just shrugged.

Matt's mouth turned down. "Well, I'm going to prove I didn't."

He grabbed his flashlight and shined it into the filing cabinet. He took out a bill and showed it to us. It was a power bill addressed to a residence in Wichita.

I didn't want to make Matt skittish, but there were three of us and only one of him. "I heard you let Patrick borrow some money."

He looked up. "Yeah, that was about eight years ago."

"Do you know why he needed it?"

"Darcy had to have surgery. Their insurance wouldn't cover it, so Patrick begged me for a loan. As much as I disliked Patrick, I didn't want Darcy to go without the care she needed, so I agreed."

Boyd pointed his finger at Matt. "And he never paid you back, so you killed him."

Matt frowned. "No! He actually paid me back, with interest, and before our agreed date."

I moved my mouth from side to side. "I thought Patrick owed money to a mob boss or something."

"Who told you that?"

"No one, but from what I was told, I came to that conclusion. That or he was gambling."

"No, and I know he really paid medical bills with it. He showed me the invoices."

"I need to call Jett," I said, pulling out my phone.

Matt shut the filing cabinet. "If you do, he's going to come arrest me."

"I'm still not sure you're innocent. That isn't why I want to call him, though. I need to ask him to check on Gene Fletcher to see who he is."

"Do we search the house?" José asked.

"I've been through everything," Matt said. "Nothing caught my attention until the filing cabinet."

"I'm going to take a picture of one of the address," I said, pulling out my phone. Matt shined his light on the bill, and I snapped a picture. It was a little dark, but it would do. "I'll just show this to Jett when I see him."

"Can you let me leave first?" Matt asked. "I know he'll come after me."

I tapped my fingers against my leg. "I don't think that's a good idea."

"But I'm innocent."

"And running makes you look guilty. I think you should turn yourself in and wait for us to figure it all out."

He took a deep breath. "I don't mean to sound doubtful, but you want me to leave my fate in the hands of two diner workers and Boyd? I remember when I was a boy, and Boyd led our scout group. He told us there was no way to prove the world was round unless NASA let all of us go up into space to see for ourselves."

Boyd chuckled. "I still stand by that statement."

"We're going to figure it out," I said. "We've done it before."

"Yeah, but doing something once doesn't make you an expert."

"Sheriff Malone is working on it as well."

"And I like Jett, but that's still putting a lot of trust out there."

"Turning yourself in would be a matter of trust. I know it's difficult, but do you really want to spend your life on the run?"

He was quiet for a minute. I wished I could see his face better, but everything was covered in shadows.

"Alright," Matt said, "but I want you to hurry. If you sit around making cookies all day, that won't do me any good."

"I think we're getting close."

He sighed. "Okay, let's go turn me in."

"Jett is still at the festival. He has to stay until it ends at midnight."

José started for the door. "Boyd and I can stay with Matt at the sheriff's office while you go find him at the festival. I'm sure he can leave for this. They had a lot of police walking around."

I dropped the three of them off at Jett's office and drove to the festival. A lot of people were in town, so he might be hard to find. People were still dancing and browsing the booths, and it didn't look like anyone was going to stop anytime soon. I stayed in my car and texted Jett, telling him where I was.

I thought about what Matt said about hurrying. If he turned himself in and was placed in jail, I would focus everything on finding the murderer. It wouldn't be fair to leave him there if he was innocent, and I leaned toward thinking he was.

There was a tap on the window, and I rolled it down. Jett leaned in, resting his arm above the window, and smiled. "You came back."

"Matt is at your office."

His smile dropped. "By himself?"

"He's with Boyd and José."

"You caught him?"

"Not exactly. We ran into him and talked him into turning himself in."

"Where was he?"

I paused, not wanting to admit where we had been.

"Ivy? Where were you?"

"At Karl's house."

"Doing what?"

"Trying to find evidence."

He sighed. "And Matt was there? What was he doing?"

"The same thing."

"Did you find anything?"

"Matt did."

"That's convenient for him."

I turned off the car engine. "I don't think he planted it. He was going through a filing cabinet when I caught him. There are a bunch of bills and stuff in there. They are all addressed to a Gene Fletcher."

He rubbed his chin. "I'm never going to get my truck out of here. It's blocked in. Can you take me to my office?"

"Yep, climb in." The night air coming in the window was making it cold. I hadn't gotten Jett's jacket back from Boyd. I hoped Jett didn't notice.

He climbed into the passenger's seat and buckled his seat belt. "Did you lose my jacket?"

Chapter 19

I woke up early the following morning to make pump-kin cookies. If I could finish them, I could spend the rest of the day trying to solve this case. Jett had grilled Matt late into the night and then let him go with instructions to stay in town.

Before doing anything else, I needed to return to Karl's house to get Jett's jacket. Boyd said he might have dropped it, but he couldn't remember. I sifted the dry ingredients into the mixer and turned it on. There was enough pumpkin pie to last the day, and we had enough pre-made desserts that no one would miss me.

Creepers had left a dead mouse by my door last night, and I was still grossed out from cleaning that up. He'd looked so proud, and the internet told me to praise him, so I did. Having a cat was one of the best things that had ever happened to me. Sure, the litter box was gross, but it was nice to have a friend who couldn't wait to see you all the time.

I separated the dough into two bowls and mixed chocolate chips into one of them. I'd learned that, much to my disbelief, there were people out there who didn't like chocolate chips in their pumpkin desserts.

I heard a key turning in the back lock, and José came in. "You're working early," he said, looking into the bowls.

"Yes, I need to get Jett's jacket from Karl's and maybe look around a bit more."

"Not by yourself, I hope?"

"Don't worry, I have my self-defense hairpin in today." We both laughed. "Besides, Karl is out of town."

"Well, make sure you come back for dinner. It's our first day with Fettuccine Alfredo on the menu."

"I'm excited."

José winked. "You should be. Why don't you go now? I'll keep watch on the cookies."

"That would be great, thank you." I took off my apron and hairnet and washed my hands. José got to work scooping the cookies onto a pan, and I grabbed my purse and left.

The drive to Karl's house wasn't long, but I noticed a vehicle behind me. I didn't want anyone to know where I was going, so I drove around town for a while. The truck stayed behind me. I glanced back to see if it looked familiar, but all I could tell was that it was black. Black was a common enough truck color, but I would almost bet it was Jett. I pulled over and waited for him to catch up. He stopped behind me and got out.

I rolled down my window and waited for him. "Was I speeding?"

He smiled. "I knew you would be out looking for trouble today, so I thought I would follow you."

"What makes you think I'm looking for trouble?"

"Statistical probability. Can I get in?"

"Sure."

He went around the car and got in. "So I have some news. I called the place Karl supposedly works at, and, of course, it wasn't open yet. After a lot of searching, I got ahold of the owner, and he's never heard of Karl Lattmire. He did me a favor and checked all the old employee records, and there was no Karl."

"Wow. He's just been living here for years under a false name?"

"It looks that way. He said he's never heard of Gene Fletcher either. I did a search for Karl Lattmire and didn't find any. After that, I searched for Gene Fletcher. There are quite a few, and one who works at the Wichita prison. What do you take from that?"

I put my hands on the steering wheel and leaned forward. "Wow. I don't know exactly."

"Maybe now would be a good time to tell me what you are keeping from me."

I turned and looked at him. It was probably time. "When I went to the prison and visited Quinn, something about him was off."

"I don't doubt it."

"Not the way you would think. He was a lot less scary than Patrick. He cared an awful lot about what Darcy and Netty were doing. I am almost convinced he isn't Quinn. He's Patrick."

Jett blinked twice. "That is not what I expected you to say."

"He also had a scar by his eye. Darcy said Patrick has one. I don't know how it happened, but somehow Patrick and Quinn switched places. He wouldn't admit it to me, but he teared up. He's worried about Darcy. I think someone is threatening him, and he's staying in prison to protect his family."

Jett shook his head. "And Gene Fletcher works at the prison. Karl must be in on it, whether or not he is Gene Fletcher. He must have been working with Quinn in some way, and he is the threat Patrick is worried about."

I nodded. I'd expected Jett to doubt my theory. "Now that Quinn is probably dead, it seems like Patrick could come clean. He didn't, so I assume things are still being hidden."

"Where were you headed just now? It seemed like you were driving around aimlessly."

I grinned. "I noticed someone following me, so I might have freaked out a little."

He smiled back. "Well, I'm glad you're at least being cautious."

"I was actually going back to Karl's house to get your jacket. Boyd was holding it, and he must have dropped it."

"I don't want you going over there. I'll go get it."

I nodded. "It's probably under one of the windows. If it's inside, it would either be in the entryway or in the first room off the entryway."

"Alright. I'll go right now, then I'll meet you at the diner at noon. If you get a chance, maybe you can search for Gene Fletcher online. I was running out of time when I did it. You might be able to find a picture or something."

I wanted to beam. Jett was giving me an assignment, which meant he valued my help. "Sounds good."

I went back to the diner and up to my room. Searching for a picture of someone who worked at the prison should be easy. I grabbed my laptop and sat on the bed. Creepers jumped up and sat at my side, his head resting on my lap. I typed in "Gene Fletcher" and watched all the results appear.

I let out a slow breath. There were more results than I'd thought. A lot of them were for people named Eugene Fletcher, but I assumed I could rule them out. If his bills said Gene, then that was probably his given name. I scrolled through some pictures with no luck. I went back into the search bar and typed "Gene Fletcher, Wichita prison." The first thing to pop up was a picture of Karl Lattmire.

"Aha. We got him, Creepers."

Creepers looked up at me with disinterest. I scratched his head and got him a treat before I headed downstairs with my laptop. I smiled at all the customers as I made my way to the kitchen. José, Anton, and Darcy were all busy cooking. Darcy had come back earlier than she'd planned now that she knew Patrick was alive.

I didn't want to say anything in front of Anton, so I just stuck my laptop in José's face. His eyes went wide. He motioned for me to follow him outside. "I'll be back in a minute," he said. "Anton, will you take the enchiladas out of the oven when they beep?"

"Sure thing, boss," Anton said from where he was cooking a burger.

We went out back, and I grinned at José. "Boss?"

He shrugged. "I told him I'm not the boss, but he keeps calling me that. Sorry."

"No, I think it fits. You are the one keeping things running around here. So what do you think about Karl?"

"That's crazy. It makes sense, though. I've been trying to figure out how Patrick and Quinn could have switched places. An insider made the most sense, but I couldn't figure out who or why someone would help him. I'm still confused about the why."

"Me too. I bet this is enough to get him arrested, even if we don't know his relationship with Quinn."

"Can you get arrested for going under a false name?"

"If you're doing it to con people, you can. Of course, we can't prove he was conning anyone except for telling them the wrong name. How long has Karl lived here?"

"I don't know. Maybe ten years."

"And how long has Quinn been in prison?"

"I don't know. I never met him. Patrick wasn't from Muddy Creek, and I never saw anyone from his family."

"Patrick and Quinn must look really similar, or someone at the prison would have noticed the switch."

The door opened, and Darcy came out. She crossed her arms against the wind. "Did you learn anything new?"

"Karl Lattmire is a guard at the prison, and his real name is Gene Fletcher," I said. "I think we are getting really close to figuring this out."

"Gene Fletcher," she muttered, wrinkling her forehead. "Why does that sound familiar?"

"Do you know how long Quinn was in prison?" I asked.

"I'm not sure. Maybe eleven or twelve years. Well, six or seven, if you aren't counting the time Patrick must have been there."

José rubbed his chin. "Do you have pictures of Quinn? We were just thinking it's odd no one at the prison noticed the switch. They must look a lot alike."

She shook her head. "I've only seen one picture at Patrick's parents' house. It was a picture of Quinn and Patrick in high school. They looked like twins. Patrick said people never believed them when they said they weren't."

I closed the laptop. With luck, this entire thing would be wrapped up in a day or two. "Did Patrick have a beard?"

"Not usually. Right before he disappeared, he'd been growing one for a month or so." She put a hand to her mouth. "Oh my. I bet he knew something before he went missing. For the last month, he was strange. He was stressed and tired all the time. He couldn't sleep. I thought little of it because his work gets stressful now and then. Someone called him several times, and he would go outside and talk. Afterward, he would pace around for a while before he came back in."

"Karl must have been threatening him already."

Darcy nodded. "I think you're right. I'm not great at remembering details, but I remember something about a sticky note on his briefcase with a phone number and a name. The name might have been Gene Fletcher, but I wouldn't swear to it."

We all turned when we heard someone walking around the side of the diner. It was Brian Hooper. He stopped and smiled when he saw us. "So this is where all the cooks hang out." His smile dropped. "Sheriff Malone just pocket texted me. I thought I would come over and see what was going on, just in case. I didn't see him inside. Do any of you know where he is?"

Panic filled me, and I shoved my laptop into José's hands. "What do you mean pocket texted?"

"We were texting last night, so I was probably the last person he texted. I got a text that just had a jumble of letters. He must have done it by accident."

"I'll go check on him. He's at Karl's."

"You should probably—"

I wasn't listening. I was running through the diner and grabbing my purse. There was a chance I was overreacting, but I didn't care. I rushed to my car and sped down the road toward Karl's house.

Chapter 20

When I pulled up to Karl's house, I expected to see Jett's truck, but it wasn't there. I jumped out of the car and ran up to the door, pounding on it. I waited a minute, and when no one answered, I pushed it open. If Jett had been here, he hadn't locked it behind him. I pulled out my phone and dialed his number, but it went straight to voicemail.

The lights were all off, but it was easy to see since the sun shone in the windows. I went from room to room, but everything was still. I opened the bathroom and paused. The blue shower curtain was closed, and I really didn't want to move it, but I forced myself to walk over. I took a deep breath and pulled it aside. The tub was empty.

A thump above me caused me to jump. Someone or something was up there. I didn't know if Karl had a pet, but I doubted it. He wouldn't go out of town and leave it here. I left the bathroom and walked carefully up the stairs. I really hoped it wasn't Karl. If it was, I didn't know how I would explain my presence in his house.

When I heard another thump, I walked down a small hall and stopped in front of a closed door. I pressed my ear to the door and waited. Something was definitely going on in there. I turned the doorknob slowly and peeked inside. It was a bathroom. Jett was on the floor on his side, his hands and feet tied, and a cloth wrapped around his mouth. There was another rope going from his tied hands to the sink pipes.

"Jett!" I exclaimed, kneeling beside him.

He shook his head and muttered something I couldn't understand through the cloth. I worked on the knot behind his head and stopped when he flinched and groaned. "Is your head hurt?"

He nodded.

"I'll be careful." I picked out the knot and pulled the cloth away from his mouth.

"Get out of here and call the police," he said. "I don't know where Karl is."

"Call the police? You are the police."

He rolled his eyes. "Call 911 and have them send someone from Wichita."

I ignored him and began working on the knot at his ankles. If I got that one first, he could stand and get out of here. "I'm not leaving."

"I can't believe I was so careless. Karl snuck up behind me and hit me on the back of the head with something. Is it bleeding?"

"No, I don't see anything."

"I bet I have a huge goose egg. I can barely focus my eyes."

The knot was tight. "This is all my fault. If I hadn't lost the jacket..."

"It's Karl's fault. Call for help before you do anything else. We don't want to be here with no one knowing where we are."

"José, Darcy, and Brian know I'm here. You pocket texted Brian."

"And they let you come on your own?"

"Well, I didn't wait around once Brian told us. They don't have any reason to know you're in trouble."

"Call 911."

I heard a click behind me. Jett froze. I turned to see Karl standing in the doorway with a gun.

"Leave her alone," Jett said, turning his head.

"I really wish you all would mind your own business," Karl said. "I'm not a violent man by nature, but you're forcing my hand."

"You better stop now," I said, getting to my feet. "Don't make it worse."

Karl's brows came together. "Killed Quinn? You mean Patrick."

"Listen to her," Jett said. "We know you somehow helped Quinn and Patrick switch places, and we know you're really Gene Fletcher."

"Well, good for you," he said, not taking his gun off me. "And now I have to figure out what to do with the two of you."

"Why kill Quinn?"

"Because he was going to blow everything. He shouldn't have come here."

"Blow it how?" I asked. I had to keep him talking while I came up with a plan.

"Quinn stole a lot of money before he was finally arrested. We became friends while he was locked up. He told me he still had the money hidden, so we made a plan. Quinn and I strategized for a long time. I moved to Muddy Creek and started carpooling with Patrick. He never saw it coming. I told Patrick I was part of the Mafia and we would kill Darcy if he didn't switch. He was shocked, of course, but he agreed."

"But how did you switch them?" I asked.

He chuckled. "I made him grow his beard to look like Quinn. I got him an orange jumpsuit and had him hide in the weeds by the highway. Quinn was assigned to clean the road with a bunch of other inmates. I was supervising, so I distracted everyone. Quinn disappeared into the brush, and Patrick came out. No one suspected."

"That's pretty low."

He shrugged. "I guess. It was a lot of money, though."

"Why kill Quinn?" Jett asked.

"When Ivy started snooping, I told Quinn. He decided to come here and make sure nothing came of it. I knew if anyone caught sight of him, it was over. He wouldn't listen. That night, I overheard him arguing with Matt Hooper. I figured if I got rid of Quinn, the blame would naturally go to Matt. I never liked Matt."

I thought about telling him more people knew he was guilty, but I didn't want him going after José and Boyd.

"I don't want to kill you two, but I'm going to have to do something. I'm pretty sure the people of Muddy Creek would believe the sheriff and the pretty diner owner ran off together. I just need to take time to think, and then I'll decide what I want to do. I know some people who wouldn't mind getting rid of the two of you." He opened a door and pointed inside. "Get in, Ivy."

I glanced at Jett and then walked in. It was a small room with a toilet. If I put my arms out, I could touch every wall. Who gave their toilet its own room? Karl grabbed my purse and slammed the door. I heard the lock turn. Forget the toilet having its own room. Who has a lock on the outside of the bathroom?

"Why do you have a lock on the outside?" Jett asked.

"I put it on backward. Who would have thought it would benefit me someday?" I heard him walk away. I could probably pop the lock without too much trouble, but I'd wait until I was sure he was gone. A few minutes later, I heard him come back in, then I heard a drill. My mouth turned down. He was doing something to the door.

When he finally stopped, he called through the door, "I'm leaving now! Don't worry too much. I'll be back tonight, hopefully with a friend."

Was that supposed to make me feel better? It really didn't. I listened to him shut the other door to the bathroom. He clomped down the stairs and slammed the front door. This was all my fault.

"Sorry, Jett. I should have called someone first."

"With luck, José will worry when you don't return."

I tried ramming my shoulder into the door.

"You aren't going to get through. He screwed a bunch of boards across it," Jett said. His voice sounded strained. I would almost bet he was trying to break free. "Is there a window in there?"

"No. Just a toilet and a plunger." I looked at the ceiling, but all that was up there was a light and a vent. And not the type of vent a person in a movie would climb through, so it was no help.

I went to the side of the toilet and focused on the opposite wall. This would be a lot easier if I had some space. There was only about eight inches between the wall and toilet on each side. I pressed my back against the wall and brought up one foot and kicked the opposite wall with my heel.

"What are you doing in there?" Jett asked.

The wall didn't even crack. I ignored Jett and kicked again in the same place, but harder. I smiled. A crack was going in a circle, slightly bigger than my foot. I kicked again and again. On the fourth kick, my foot broke through. "Yes!" I yanked my foot out and started pulling at the drywall. If Karl caught me, he was going to be mad.

"Ivy? Be careful."

"Don't worry," I said, pulling away a sizable chunk. I was going to have to do a lot more to fit through. I kicked it again, right next to the hole, and it broke easily. I worked for a good few minutes on the hole and then started on the outer wall. It was harder to kick through because it was deeper, and my foot kept getting caught.

After what felt like forever, my foot broke through. At the same moment, I heard a crash on the other side of the wall. "Whoa!" Jett exclaimed. I freed my foot and looked through the hole and down at Jett. The pipes from the sink were on the ground, and he was pulling his ropes around them. It didn't look easy with his hands tied behind him.

"What did you do?" I asked.

"Pipes aren't that strong. I just yanked on them a few times, and they broke."

Standing, I kicked at the wall again until the hole was much bigger. I continued kicking the wall until I had two decent-sized holes between the studs. I pushed out a few pieces, then pushed myself through. It was tight, but I managed it. There was probably dust from the drywall on my head, but I didn't care.

"Do you want to hop, or should I try to untie your feet?" I asked.

He had freed himself of the pipes but was still on the floor. "I'm not sure I can hop down the stairs without falling."

I got down and pried at the knot. I pulled my "self-defense" hair pin from my hair and stuck it into the knot. It took a lot of wiggling, but I finally got it loose. I grabbed one of his arms and helped him to his feet.

"We can worry about my hands later," he said. "Let's get out of here." We rushed through the house and out the door. "Where's my truck?"

"My car is gone as well," I said. "That complicates everything. At least he lives in town."

"He took my wallet, keys, and gun. I feel like such an idiot. I can't believe he took me down."

"Don't feel bad. Anyone can be surprised. Besides, he's a prison guard. He's going to be fit. Come on. We need to get to a place with people in case he finds us again."

We made it back to the diner and went around back. We burst into the kitchen, and José, Darcy, and Anton all turned to us.

José was mixing something. "Oh good, you're back. I was about to come looking for you." He took in my appearance. "What happened to you?"

"Karl happened. Can you help me untie Jett?"

José's eyes went wide, and he rushed over to Jett. He studied the knot. "Let me get a knife." He went to a drawer and came back with a steak knife. "Don't move." He sawed at the rope, and it fell to the floor.

Jett rubbed his wrists. "Thanks."

Anton stood frozen, and Darcy looked like she might cry.

"Can I use someone's cell phone?" Jett asked. José unlocked his and handed it to him.

"Thanks."

We all sat quietly while Jett called the police in Wichita and asked for some officers to come help. He gave them a few details and hung up.

Boyd came barrelling into the kitchen. "Karl is walking toward the diner!"

Chapter 21

"What do we do?" Darcy asked.

Boyd shrugged. "Go question him."

José grinned. "You are so far behind."

Boyd scratched his head. "What are you talking about?"

"There isn't time," Jett said. "Everyone wait here and see what he does." He picked up José's rolling pin. It seemed like a sad substitution for his gun.

The diner door flew open, and Karl raced in. "Hey, everyone!" he bellowed. The diner went quiet as all the customers turned to see what was happening. "I just passed the sheriff and Ivy Clark. They said they were finished with Muddy Creek and all its problems. The sheriff said Matt Hooper killed Patrick Henderson, and he's tired of cleaning up our messes."

Jett arched his brow. "Pathetic. That's the best he can come up with?"

I peeked out of the corner of the kitchen window. Barbra stood and walked toward Karl. She put her hands on her hips. "There's not a one of us in here who wouldn't like to see the sheriff and Ivy run off together, but I don't believe it. They are both too reliable to leave their responsibilities."

Karl puffed out his chest. "Why would I lie about something like that?"

Barbra poked him in the shoulder with her finger. "That's what I'd like to know. I've always thought there was something wrong with you."

Jett came up to my side and whispered, "Can you see if he has the gun?"

"I can't tell," I whispered back.

"What's wrong with you people?" Karl asked. "Someone needs to call the police and have Matt arrested."

"Darcy, stay here," Jett said. I turned to see Darcy burst through the door and charge at Karl with a heavy wooden cutting board. Jett took off after her. I stood and watched as Darcy swung at a stunned Karl and hit him in the head.

Before Karl could recover, Jett grabbed him and threw him to the floor. He sat on his back and pulled his arms behind him.

"Get off!" Karl yelled.

Jett struggled to get him to hold still. "Karl Lattmire, or should I say Gene Fletcher, you are under arrest for the murder of Quinn Henderson. Ivy, will you go get me some rope or something? He took my handcuffs back at the house."

I ran into the kitchen and returned with a roll of twine and a pair of scissors. I unrolled a long piece and tied it around Karl's hands while Jett held them.

Barbra clapped, and the rest of the diner patrons joined in. "I don't know what just happened, but I'm glad to have witnessed it," she said. "Who the heck is Quinn Henderson?"

It felt like an eternity as we waited for the Wichita police to come and take Karl away. After clearing out the diner, Jett kept a sharp eye on him. Jett had gone out and talked to the police for a while, then came back when they drove away.

José, Darcy, Boyd, and I sat at a booth waiting for him. He strolled to the booth and scooted in next to me. "I'm going to have to go in and deal with this. Ivy, you need to come make a statement."

I was exhausted, and my wall-kicking leg throbbed. "Right now?"

"Soon. It needs to be today."

Darcy leaned forward. "What about Patrick?"

"Someone at the prison is checking his fingerprints, just to be sure. I think they'll let him go."

She stood. "Then I'm going. I'll just call my mom and let her know I'll be late."

"I can go tell her what happened," Boyd offered. "That way, I can stay and help with Netty if she needs it. I'll take Creepers. Netty likes cats."

Darcy smiled. "That would be great, thanks."

I wasn't sure how I felt about Netty with Creepers, but I trusted Boyd.

"I'll stay and clean up," José said. "I hope Anton comes back tomorrow. He looked a little shaken."

"How are we going to get to Wichita?" I asked. "We don't know where our vehicles are."

Jett moved his jaw from side to side. "They can't be far. Let's go look." We all got to our feet and went our separate ways. Jett and I walked back to Karl's house, and Jett studied the ground.

"It's too bad he doesn't live on a muddy road. Then we could just follow the tire tracks," he said.

I scanned the scenery. "How long were you in the house after he tied you up?"

"About a half hour."

"So he could have taken your truck thirty minutes away."

"I doubt it. He got to the diner pretty quick after leaving us here. He would have had to get rid of your car pretty fast."

"Well, I'm guessing he didn't go deeper into town, so let's go that way." He pointed down the road.

"On foot?"

He grinned. "Unless you have a better idea."

We started walking in silence. The farther we went, the more my leg hurt, but I tried to keep up.

"What's down this road?" I asked.

"The pond. It's just around that bend up there."

I stopped. "You don't suppose he dumped our vehicles in the pond, do you?"

He shrugged. "I wouldn't be surprised. It's the closest place I can think of to ditch something like that."

"Oh boy. How deep is it?"

"Deep enough to cover a truck. I haven't measured it or anything."

"I love that car."

"Are you alright? You're walking funny."

I smiled. "I guess my wall-kicking muscles aren't used to being used. It's fine. I just hope we don't have to go much farther."

"We should have invested in some electric bikes like Boyd."

We went around a corner and turned onto a small dirt road that led down to a large pond. If no one had called it a pond, I would call it a small lake. I searched the ground for tire tracks but couldn't find anything.

Jett sighed and draped an arm over my shoulders. "Well, I guess that is that."

"What?" I asked, looking over the pond.

"Right there." He pointed. "It's my truck antenna."

I squinted. "Oh, I see it." The black antenna poked out from about thirty feet into the water. "I bet my car is there, too. You know I've only been here for a handful of months, and I've lost two cars?"

He rubbed my shoulder. "At this rate, you'll go through at least two more this year."

"Ha ha. Now what?"

"I'll make some more calls and get them pulled out. They might be okay. I'll also call my parents and ask them to let me borrow one of their cars. We should have driven with Darcy."

"I can call Darcy and see if she's gone yet."

"I'd rather have my own way home. Who knows how long everything will take?"

"Do you still have José's phone?"

He smacked his palm on his forehead. "I forgot Karl took my phone. I bet he threw it in the truck."

I moved out from under his arm, even though I didn't want to. "Well, let's get walking."

I focused on going forward and tried to ignore my leg.

"You know, you should go to the academy and become my deputy," Jett said.

I laughed. "I would be a terrible deputy."

"You'd be great. You've solved as many crimes as you've lost cars."

"I had a lot of help. In the end, you and Darcy took him down."

"But you figured it all out. I never would have gone and talked to Quinn, and if I had, I'm not sure I would have questioned him the way you did, so I wouldn't have figured out he was really Patrick. I didn't think Quinn had anything to do with anything."

"I guess I'm just nosy."

"No, you were helping a friend. But you need to be more careful. You're lucky a lot of things worked out the way they did."

"If I was more careful, you might still be tied up in Karl's bathroom."

He ran a hand through his hair. "That's true. Thanks for busting us out of there."

I grinned. "I never imagined myself breaking through a wall like that."

"You're pretty amazing."

I could feel the temperature in my face go up about a hundred degrees. "So do you have any more unsolved cases you want me to take on?"

"No. I think we need to go to Wichita, get that all over with, then you should go home, cuddle your cat, and read a good book. Sleep for a few days, then go back to running your diner."

"That sounds nice. What about you? Do you get a break after something like this?"

"Not until we get more law around here, but I'm fine."

"You need some fun in your life."

He smiled. "Isn't that what I've been having?"

"You think getting tied up and lying on Karl's floor is fun?"

"No. I wouldn't say no to another dance at the festival this Saturday."

I smiled. "Neither would I."

Chapter 22

I pulled my famous chocolate chip cookies from the oven and frowned. They were completely flat. I must have over-mixed them. It was the first time this month I'd made cookies without pumpkin, and I'd failed. I placed them on the counter and glared at them.

José leaned over my shoulder. "Well, those look... fun."

I smacked him in the shoulder with my oven mitt. "Now what?"

"People don't need cookies and pie. It's fine with just pie."

"But we're celebrating Patrick's homecoming! It needs to be perfect!"

"It will be. Just add some more flour to the next batch."

I placed the mixing bowl back on the mixer and added more flour. It had been a long three days. Karl was locked away, and Patrick had been released. I thought my car was a goner, but a mechanic had dried it out, then cleaned it, making sure everything still worked. Jett's truck was running as well. When I got in the car, I felt like I could smell fish, but I think it might be in my head.

Darcy and Patrick sat in a booth together. I hadn't seen her release his hand since they'd come in. Netty kept shooting them both dirty looks, but they ignored them. She probably didn't remember Patrick. She'd only been three when he went missing. Patrick had cut his hair and shaved, making him look a lot more like the picture Darcy had shown me.

Jett had only gotten home last night. He'd had a lot to do with wrapping things up. The police had talked to me, and I would probably have to testify in a few months at Karl's trial. I knew his name was really Gene, but I kept thinking of him as Karl. It also sounded like Jett might get a deputy. He needed one, but I wasn't sure how I felt about it. I knew how Jett worked. A deputy might be completely different.

Karl refused to say what he did with the body, but Jett was confident he would eventually tell—something to do with a plea bargain. I wasn't so sure.

I scooped dough into pans and hoped they would turn out. From the consistency, I could tell that they wouldn't be as good as usual. I went out into the main room to wait for the timer.

"Hello, everyone," I said loudly. The talking died down, and the patrons turned to me. "Thank you all for coming." I looked around at all the familiar and unfamiliar faces. We had a nice turnout. "It's great to be able to welcome Patrick home." Everyone clapped. "We are doing this buffet style, so feel free to come up to the bar and scoop up what you want."

Patrick stood. "Can I say something? I want to thank Ivy Clark for not giving up, even when I told her to. Thanks to her and Sheriff Malone, I'm home with my family."

"Hey! José and I helped too," Boyd said, with a teasing smile. He was sitting at a table with Barbra, Opal, and Jett.

Patrick nodded. "Yes, thanks to everyone who helped. I feel so blessed to be with my family again." Netty sighed and stuck her forehead on the table. Patrick was going to have to be patient with that relationship. I wondered if he was allowed to call her Netty.

"Everyone, eat!" I said. I was wearing my neon cat apron. I hoped Jett noticed.

Darcy came up behind me and gave me a quick hug. "I'm never going to be able to thank you enough."

I smiled. "I'm just happy I could help. It makes me happy to know we made a difference. I thought Patrick's parents would come."

Her brow rose. "They said they don't do events with more than five people. They were happy to see him, though. We spent all day at their house yesterday. After we caught up for a few minutes, they made him watch *Ghostbusters*." She laughed. "I guess they thought after five years in jail, he must miss it."

"Your mom didn't want to come?"

She rolled her eyes. "No. I think she's secretly annoyed that Patrick is back. She hates coming to town. She has too many health problems to live on her own, and Patrick and I decided to buy a house and let her come if she wants. That way, it's our house, and she can't boss me around all the time. We're putting in an offer on a house in Wichita."

"I'm happy for you, but we'll miss you. It's too bad Sally doesn't like to talk to anyone."

"Yeah, she always tells me she doesn't need to leave the house when she can get anyone to come do what she needs."

I laughed. "She told me that." My smile slipped as I recalled my last conversation with Sally. Something was nagging at the back of my brain.

Darcy's brows came together. "Are you alright?"

"Yes, I just remembered something."

"Well, I'm going to go get some pie. Thanks again."

I went into the kitchen and pulled the cookies from the oven. This batch looked a lot better. Jett came in, and I rushed to him. I grabbed his sleeve and pulled him farther from the door.

"What is it?" he asked.

"Probably nothing, but I just had a thought. The last time I talked to Sally Peterson, she said Karl did some work in her crawl space. Karl doesn't take me as a help your crabby neighbor type."

Jett's eyes widened. "You think Karl hid Quinn's body in the crawl space?"

"Maybe."

He grinned. "Let's go." He grabbed my hand and pulled me through the diner.

"José, you're in charge," I said as we hurried out.

Barbra laughed. "It's about time those two ran off together."

My cheeks burned, but I kept going. I climbed into Jett's truck and buckled up. I was shaking a little, but that seemed ridiculous. There wasn't any danger anymore, and I'd made it through all of that fine.

Jett slammed the door and turned and gave me a half smile. "You ready for this?"

"I'm nervous for some reason."

He turned the key and backed up. "You don't have to go into the crawl space."

"Do you smell fish, or is it just me? Every time I get in my car now, I feel like it smells."

He sniffed. "All I smell is you."

"Thanks a lot."

He laughed. "You smell like vanilla."

I relaxed. I could deal with that. The closer we got to Sally's, the more nervous I became. I wondered what we would say to Sally. She would be mad if it turned out there was a body under her house. There was a chance I was wrong, but I felt almost certain I wasn't.

Jett pulled into the driveway and reached over to squeeze my hand. "You can stay here if you want."

"No, I'm coming." I climbed out of the truck, and we walked up to the house. Sally was sitting on the porch again.

Her eyes narrowed as we came closer. "What is with you people dropping by all the time? With how far technology has come, I would think you might at least call or text."

Jett grinned. "It's good to see you too, Sally."

"I hope you aren't here to try to get me to go to town for that celebration."

"You might have fun," I said.

"Nope."

Jett climbed the steps to the top of the porch. "That isn't why we're here. Do you mind if we look in your crawl space?"

She picked up a bottle of what I assumed was alcohol and took a long drink, her eyes not leaving Jett. She placed it back down and glared. "Why would you want to do that?"

"You said Karl did some work in your crawl space. We think he might have hidden Quinn's body down there."

"That's ridiculous. He wouldn't have gotten past without me seeing."

He tilted his head. "You watched him the entire time?"

"Of course I did. I will not have someone in my house and not watch them."

"Can I look?"

"No."

"Why not?"

"Because I don't like people in my house."

I wasn't sure Jett was going to win this one. Sally looked determined to keep us out.

"I guess I can get a warrant and come back."

Sally pressed her lips together. "Ivy can go look."

I swallowed. I was up for a lot when it came to solving a mystery, but going into a dark crawl space with who knew what types of creatures and possibly a body was almost past my limits.

Jett looked at me. "What do you think?"

"I suppose I can look."

Sally came slowly to her feet, and we followed her into the house. She opened a coat closet and pointed at the floor. "It's under that carpet. Just pull it aside."

Jett pulled the carpet back to reveal a square trapdoor. He lifted it open and glanced inside. It was dark.

"Do it quick," Sally said. "You don't want to spend too much time down there. I bet they're all kinds of bugs and snakes."

A chill ran down my spine. "Snakes?"

Jett shook his head. "I doubt there are snakes in there." He didn't say anything about the bugs.

"How deep is it?" I asked, shining my phone flashlight down.

"Not too deep," Sally said. "When Karl went in, it only went to his chest."

I sighed and sat on the floor. "Keep a light coming down." Jett grabbed his flashlight and flipped it on. I took a deep breath and put my legs in the hole. It wasn't very big. I put both hands on the sides and lowered myself down. When my feet hit the floor, I was still head and shoulders above the ground.

I pulled my head down and crouched. I shined my light around. The ground below me was dirt, with some wooden beams and wires. I couldn't make sense of it, so I walked around, studying the ground. Jett had his arm dropped into the opening, shining his light.

The ground was different in one spot. It was packed down but not as packed as the rest of the ground. It looked like someone had stepped all over it trying to pack it. I could make out footprints.

"Can I get a shovel?" I called.

"You can't dig down there!" Sally exclaimed. "I don't want you ruining the foundation and making the house fall!"

"I'm not going to uproot the house. An area here looks like it might have been disturbed."

"Ouch!" Jett exclaimed right as his flashlight fell to the ground. I turned to see what the problem was, but the trapdoor slammed closed. I moved as fast as I could without bumping my head and shined the light above.

I pushed on the trapdoor, and nothing happened. I could hear my heart pounding in my ears. The thought of never getting out of here was terrifying,

Before I could decide what to do, it opened, and light spilled in. Jett poked his head through. "Come up."

I stuck my head through the hole and put my elbows on the floor. I tried to pull myself out, but the opening was small and awkward. Jett put his hands under my arms, and I held his shoulders. I felt like a toddler being pulled up like that, and it didn't feel good.

Sally sat on the floor, handcuffed to the coffee table leg. She scowled at us.

"What happened?" I asked.

"Sally hit me in the head with a vase. She must have thought she could knock me out or something."

"I would have if it wasn't for this blasted arthritis," she muttered. "I shouldn't be blamed for anything in my crawl space."

"You wouldn't have been," Jett said. "We know Karl was down there."

Her eyes narrowed.

"But you knew, didn't you?" I asked. "You knew he put Quinn down there."

"Not exactly. I thought it was Patrick, but I had nothing to do with killing him."

Jett crossed his arms. "Why didn't you come to me?"

"I didn't want to get in trouble."

"Did Karl threaten you?"

"No."

"Did he know you knew?"

"He might have paid me a bit not to mention it."

"How much?" Jett asked. "No use lying. I can have your bank statements checked."

She grumbled something under her breath. "About ten thousand. You can't blame me for accepting. He might have gotten violent if I hadn't. It's not like the world is missing a good, upstanding citizen. He was a criminal who should have been in jail."

"But that's not your responsibility."

"Fine, take me to prison. I don't really care. Living here, living there, it doesn't really matter to me."

Chapter 23

I curled up on my window seat with a copy of *Jane Eyre*. I was tired from the last few weeks and wanted to do something that didn't require much thought. I've read *Jane Eyre* at least ten times, and it's become comfort food for me. My copy was at my parents' house, so I'd borrowed it from the library.

Creepers jumped onto my lap and fell asleep. I'd finally tried the catnip spray on the cat tree, and Creepers had gone crazy. He'd scratched it and chewed on it and then ran around my room like a crazy cat. It was finally wearing off, and he was tired.

I've decided to expand the diner. Having a larger menu means we need a larger kitchen. There's enough space to expand out back with room to spare. I'll also expand my living space into more than just a room. There will be a sitting room and possibly a small kitchen area. I know I have the diner kitchen, but I'd like something upstairs for when I'm just cooking for myself. A small library would be nice, but I'll have to check the cost.

Sally had been taken to a rehab center, and we all hoped she could get the help she needed. Jett wasn't sure if she would be charged with assisting Karl or not. She would be charged with assaulting an officer and trying to trap me in the crawl space.

I ended up missing the last of the harvest festivals. There was just too much to do. I didn't mind, but I was a little disappointed I didn't get to dance with Jett again. I still made treats for Livy to sell, and we'd had a lot of people come into the diner to get more muffins once they got them at the festival.

Halloween had been less work than I'd thought it would be. The tradition in Muddy Creek was to have all the kids in town and the surrounding area go trick-or-treating on the town square. Everyone sat outside in a row and passed out candy. It made it easier for families. No one had to walk too far, and it didn't take long. Not many kids were around, so seeing them all out and dressed was fun.

I opened the book and got a whiff of the old pages. I know I shouldn't admit this because it goes against what most book lovers like, but I hate the smell of old books. My friend back in Arizona used to love to go to old bookstores for the smell, but I could do without it. I liked a brand new, unread book. It wasn't a deal breaker, just a preference. This book had definitely been well-loved.

I flipped through the pages, excited to read. I usually read it yearly, but I missed last year and possibly the one before. Some writing in the back made me pause. In faded blue pen, it said, "I know who killed Tabitha, and I'll take it to my grave." I stared at the page. A teenager probably wrote it thinking they were funny. I went back to the front page, and it said "Property of S. Roberts."

I didn't know anyone in the area whose last name was Roberts. I wasn't going to get worked up over a prank. How was I going to relax with something like this in the book? I put it down and grabbed a different book. *Jane Eyre* would have to wait. The next time I saw Brian, I would ask him where he got the book. Most in the library were donated.

I rubbed one hand over Creepers and tried to focus. My eyes kept going back to *Jane Eyre*. After ten minutes of reading the same page over and over, I gave up and went downstairs. I needed to take my mind off the message in the book, and I knew how. I'd been waiting for a good time to talk to José, and now was as good as any.

It was a slow time, with only one table occupied. I entered the kitchen to find him sitting on a stool, scrolling on his phone. I knew it was slow if José was on his phone. He was the hardest worker I'd ever seen, and he wouldn't stop unless everything was clean and in order. Anton wasn't scheduled until dinner today.

"Hey, José?"

He looked up. "What do you need?"

"You know how I told you about my plans to expand?"

"Yes. I think it's a good idea."

"I'm thinking of putting in an office for the manager. Just something small with a desk and computer. What do you think?"

He scratched his chin. "You're going to hire a manager?" I knew he would be supportive, but I could tell it worried him. He had things running smoothly.

I tried not to smile. "I'm thinking about it. Being in the diner is fun and I enjoy baking, but I don't like all the decisions and paperwork. I was actually wondering if you would like the job."

His eyes widened. "You want me to be the manager?"

"Yes. Only if you want to, though. You know more about what's going on than I do."

"I would love that."

I smiled. "Then you are now officially the new manager. Start by giving yourself a twenty percent raise."

José laughed and gave me a hug. "This is great. I can still cook, though, right?"

"It's up to you. You're the manager."

"This is exciting. I have a good feeling about the remodel. Now that we don't have anything else to worry about, we can focus all our attention on putting this place on the map."

I nodded, pushing the name Tabitha from my mind.

We had a good thing going here, and it would only get better. Gramma Sue would have been proud of what we'd accomplished so far. I smiled as I pictured her. She'd loved this place, and so did most of the people in the town. It was a beautiful legacy.

Pumpkin Chocolate Chip Muffins

3 1/3 cups flour

2 cups sugar

2 T pumpkin spice

1 tsp baking soda

1 tsp baking soda

1/2 tsp salt

4 eggs

1 can pumpkin puree (30 oz)

1 cup chocolate chips

Mix dry ingredients. Add eggs and mix. Stir in pumpkin puree. Mix in chocolate chips. Bake at 350 degrees for 30 minutes.

About the Author

Kristy Dixon received a degree in English from the University of Utah. She started writing stories when she was seven and never stopped. She enjoys writing fantasy books for middle grade and teens and cozy mysteries. At home, she spends her time playing board games with her husband and kids and writing. Occasionally she takes part in a Super Mario marathon. She has six chickens and a cat that help keep life amusing. If she isn't playing with her kids or writing, she is usually eating cookies, or wishing she was eating cookies.

Also By Kristy Dixon

Trapped In Once Upon a Time

Made in the USA
Monee, IL
20 February 2025

12659253R00121